"I don't know how you do it with two of them and only one of you." Jason exhaled heavily and plopped the paper towels into the cart.

"I manage. Normally, my shopping wouldn't take this long, but we had a lot of extra food to buy."

"Told you Scott and I cleaned out the cupboards." He frowned. "You look about ready to drop."

"I'm tired," Layne admitted.

"All right, then let's get you back home." He took the cart from her and went in the direction of the checkout counter.

No matter what she had said to her friends about Jason leaving soon, this everyday trip to the store had left her daydreaming of what their life might have been like if he had never left. Their few days together had offered her a taste. But along with the daydreams had come a fear big enough to eclipse all the pleasure she had felt.

She was getting too comfortable with Jason again. Was being reminded much too poignantly of the boy she used to love.

The boy who had stopped loving her.

Dear Reader,

Ever since I was a little girl, I've loved reading series books. I began with mysteries such as The Bobbsey Twins and Encyclopedia Brown, then moved on to The Hardy Boys and Nancy Drew. Once I fell in love with romance, writing a series of books seemed like the perfect fit for me.

Often, my series are tied together by place, and I've loved being able to return to my small towns of Dillon, Texas, and Flagman's Folly, New Mexico. With the Hitching Post Hotel series, I'm thrilled to have many opportunities to come back to Cowboy Creek, New Mexico. But in case you're wondering, my series are always stand-alone books. Though a hero or heroine may appear in other stories, they reach their happy-ever-after by the end of their book. Because that's why we read romance, isn't it?

Whether you're a frequent visitor to the Hitching Post Hotel or dropping by for the first time, I hope you enjoy your visit. In this story, Grandpa Jed may have run out of granddaughters to marry off, but he's still in the matchmaking business! And he's facing his toughest challenge to date with Jason and Layne, who were once married and divorced...from each other.

I'd love to hear what you think of the books. You can get in touch through my website, barbarawhitedaille.com, or mailing address, PO Box 504, Gilbert, AZ 85299. You can also find me on Facebook and Twitter.

Until we meet again,

Barbara White Daille

COWBOY IN CHARGE

BARBARA WHITE DAILLE

HARLEQUIN® WESTERN ROMANCE®

Recycling programs
for this product may
not exist in your area.

ISBN-13: 978-0-373-75628-5

Cowboy in Charge

Copyright © 2016 by Barbara White-Rayczek

Printed in U.S.A.

Barbara White Daille and her husband still inhabit their own special corner of the wild, wild Southwest, where the summers are long and hot and the lizards and scorpions roam.

Barbara loves looking back at the short stories and two books she wrote in grade school and realizing that—except for the scorpions—she's doing exactly what she planned. She's thrilled to have published more than a dozen novels, with more in the works, and is grateful for the readers who love her stories. The awards and top reviews her books have garnered are like icing on her favorite dessert: chocolate cake.

As always, Barbara hopes you will enjoy reading her books. She would love to have you drop by for a visit at her website, barbarawhitedaille.com.

Books by Barbara White Daille

Harlequin American Romance

The Sheriff's Son
Court Me, Cowboy
Family Matters
A Rancher's Pride
The Rodeo Man's Daughter
Honorable Rancher
Rancher at Risk

The Hitching Post Hotel

The Cowboy's Little Surprise
A Rancher of Her Own
The Lawman's Christmas Proposal

Visit the Author Profile page
at Harlequin.com for more titles.

To everyone who asked to
come back to Cowboy Creek.

I hope you enjoy your return visit with
Grandpa Jed and his family and friends!

And as always, to Rich.

Chapter One

Spending his afternoon at a kid's first birthday party normally wouldn't have made it anywhere near Jason McAndry's to-do list. As this party was in honor of his buddy's little girl, he didn't have a choice.

From his seat on one of the windowsills of the screened-in back porch, he rested his beer bottle on his knee and looked through the sliding glass doors into the house.

Near the crowded dining table, the proud papa hugged his birthday girl, who was all dressed up in pink ruffles with a tiny bow in her nearly nonexistent hair. After one last kiss to her cheek, Greg handed the star of the show over to her mama.

Jason tried for a smile. The man sure did dote on his daughter.

In the three years since they'd met, he and Greg had put in a lot of miles traveling on the rodeo circuit. Back in those early days, they had both been single and fancy-free till Greg had first gotten roped by a woman, then hog-tied into becoming a daddy. Yet his buddy didn't seem to see things that way.

From that point on, their trips included frequent slide

shows as Greg thumbed through the latest photos his wife sent to his cell phone.

Jason shoved his hand into the back pocket of his jeans. His fingertips brushed the edge of his wallet. He had no photos on his phone, carried no pictures except his own on his driver's license. But in that wallet he'd tucked a now worn and permanently creased copy of another child's birth announcement.

Greg stepped out onto the porch and slid the glass door closed behind him. He frowned. "What are you doing out here, guarding the beer locker?"

He had left the house to get some space, some breathing room. But he couldn't say that. "Just came out for a refill."

Greg nodded at his half-empty bottle. "Doesn't look like you got one. Or are you ready for another already?"

"No, this one's still good. And I'll be driving soon." He moved to sit in one of the wooden porch benches and set the bottle on the wide arm. "Take a load off. All this master of ceremonies stuff must wear you out."

"Never." Greg took a nearby chair. "I've got lots of lost time to make up for."

He meant his absence this season when they had been on the road, competing in rodeos across the country. Mere weeks away in total, while by comparison, Jason hadn't been back to his hometown in years. He didn't want to consider why or how he'd left Cowboy Creek. Yet, lately, both had been taking up too much space in his thoughts.

"We're talking about me hanging up my spurs," Greg said quietly.

"Giving up rodeo?" He might have done the same at one point. Now he couldn't imagine making that choice.

But Greg had his family to come back to. He had… himself.

Inside the house, both sides of Greg's family had gathered around his wife and little girl, all of them making too much noise for them to overhear this conversation, even with the windows wide-open on this mild January day. But, like his buddy, he kept his voice low. "You really want to leave your share of the winnings to me?"

Greg laughed. "Yeah, I wouldn't mind. You're welcome to them. I don't want to miss out on any more of my daughter's life. And we want more kids. Soon, not down the road." He swallowed a mouthful of beer, then continued, "Do you ever regret what happened with you and your wife?"

He stiffened. The question had come out of nowhere. Sure, he'd told Greg a long time ago that he'd gotten divorced before he'd hit the rodeo trail. What he hadn't told him was that had come to pass partly *because* of his refusal to hang up his spurs. That was only one item on a long list of his ex-wife's grievances.

After that lone conversation, he and Greg had never discussed it again. He had a feeling he knew why his buddy had brought it up now. "Listen, you may be settling into a rut as an old married man, but don't go getting any ideas about me joining you in the trenches."

"There's a lot to be said about having a family to come home to."

"Yeah, and there's a lot I *don't* need to say about that." On that long-ago night over a few too many beers, he had told Greg all about the girl he'd left behind. The high-school-sweetheart-turned-wife who'd turned against him after their last rip-roaring fight. The wife who had wound up kicking him out of their apartment, the only place that had ever felt like home to him. He should have known better than to expect that to last. "Best day of my life, when I started following the rodeo."

"I thought that, too, once upon a time."

He rolled his eyes and exhaled heavily. "And if you're planning to practice your storytelling skills on me, I may just take off again right now."

"Can't do that. We haven't even had the cake yet." Greg glanced into the house at the crowd around the table in the direction of a leggy redhead, one of his wife's friends. "How'd the hot date go last night?"

Jason glanced at her, too, then away again. "It went cold fast," he said shortly. He took another swig from his nearly empty bottle, partly to get the last mouthful of beer but mostly to distract Greg from more questions.

When he'd rung the doorbell of the woman's apartment last night, she had come to the door dressed to kill. Her shiny blouse wouldn't have needed more than a touch to slide right off, but the skintight leather pants sure would have required some assistance. Of course, considering her friendship with Greg's wife and the fact it was a first date, his run around those bases would have happened only in his dreams.

"That was our first and last date," he said firmly to Greg.

His interest had worn off quickly when she stepped out into the hallway. She began to pull the door closed so abruptly, she would have crushed her little boy in the gap—if Jason hadn't yelled a warning at her. In her defense, the kid had appeared out of nowhere. And that's just where she had sent him off to again.

The boy looked about five, not nearly old enough to be left alone, Jason knew. He'd been seven the first time his mother left him on his own, and even that wasn't old enough. But after the first half-dozen times, he'd toughened up fast.

Yet this woman simply gave the boy an order to step back before she closed the door. No goodbye kiss or cuddle, not even a last-minute rumpling of his hair. And without a sign of anybody else in the house.

"You want to settle him in before we leave?" he asked while they still stood outside her apartment.

"Don't worry about him. I've got a sitter."

Her offhand care of the child left him wanting to shake his head in wonder. And then to cringe in shame. Who was he to criticize? And yet, the incident had left a sour taste in his mouth. Their evening had gone downhill from there, ending in an early night. When he arrived at the party this afternoon, they had nodded at each other as if they'd just met, then went their separate ways. No problem there. He'd become an expert at moving on.

Greg eyed him. "Don't you think it might be time to forget about your ex and—"

"Long forgotten already," he said firmly.

"—find yourself another woman? This time next year, you could have a little girl or boy of your own."

"Already got one." *Dang.* He hadn't meant to blurt that out. He owed the slip to his unease over last night and to the months Greg had been preoccupied with his baby. Thoughts of his own child had been on his mind so often lately, the words had come out almost naturally.

Greg stared at him. "Well, listen to this. You picked up a woman and never said a word to me?"

Yeah, he could go with that story and continue to keep his secret to himself.

No, he couldn't. Greg wouldn't rest until he'd learned

every last thing he could about someone who didn't exist. Sighing, he admitted, "Not a woman. I meant I've got a little boy."

The other man's jaw dropped for a moment. Then he grinned. "You're kidding. How old?"

"Three."

"I don't believe this. For as long as I've known you, you've had a son, and you never thought to tell me a word about him? Not even after I started bragging about becoming a daddy?"

"Guess not."

"Obviously not. Why didn't you say something, man?"

Inside the house, Greg's little girl gave a high-pitched giggle. He could picture her a year ago in the photo on Greg's phone, all wrapped up in a pink-and-white baby blanket. He could see other views of her as she grew bigger, sprouted a little more hair, cut a couple of teeth.

Ages and stages he'd never gotten to see with his son. Thoughts he'd never had until a few months ago. Memories he'd never missed until Greg started with those danged photos.

Those memories had hit him hard last night, when his date had walked away from her child without a second look.

Her action was too similar to the thoughts he'd been dwelling on for months now. Too close to what *he* had once done to leave him in any mood for enjoying the evening. When he had left his hometown, he hadn't been a daddy yet. Hell, he still wasn't. Not in the full sense of the word. But he'd known the baby was on the way. And still, without once looking back, he'd walked away from his unborn son.

Shrugging, he looked at Greg. "What's there to say?"

"The boy's name, for starters. Who he takes after. When he was born, and where he is now."

"Back in Cowboy Creek."

"You've seen the boy?"

He shook his head.

The look on Greg's face made him wish he hadn't refused another beer. Giving his buddy the chance to play host might have derailed this entire conversation. "My wife was pregnant when we split up. I left town, and we never kept in touch."

Greg sat looking at him as if he'd just sprouted a second pair of hands. "That's not you, man. What the hell happened?"

He shrugged. "It was almost four years ago. You weren't you then, either. We've both changed since then. Both grown up. Back then I was young and stupid," he admitted, "and still too focused on the wrong things. Like having a good time and hanging out at the Cantina in Cowboy Creek with my friends. Like getting drunk and getting laid. And to hear my ex tell it, like funneling our cash reserves into any rodeo that ever happened by."

He had his reasons for wanting to enter those rodeos, for needing to win, but Layne saw the cash going toward entry fees and believed only that he was wasting money they needed for other things. "She didn't appreciate any of that, especially when she sat at home dealing with morning sickness." He laughed, trying to shrug off his guilt. "How the heck can they call it morning sickness when it seems to last all day?"

"You got me there. But that still doesn't tell me why you walked."

He grasped the neck of his beer bottle in both hands.

All these years later, the memory of that last fight still made him tense like a spring-coiled wire. "I didn't walk, at least not at first. Not until my ex threw me out."

I'd be better off without you. Layne's voice had cracked on the words but she'd stood firm, her arms crossed over her chest and her chin held high. Her eyes were bright, not with the softness of tears but with the hard flint of anger.

"We'd gotten to the point we couldn't say good morning without it leading to a fight," he admitted. "When she told me to leave, I decided I was doing the right thing by going."

"And your boy?"

Again, he shrugged. "She was only a few months pregnant. I've never laid eyes on the kid."

"But you took care of him? You sent money home?"

"Sure, I did. Every month. And every month the envelope came back marked 'return to sender.'" And the sight of Layne's handwriting on every envelope that came in the mail acted like acid on an old burn, opening up the same wound.

You've left me alone one too many times, she had said the night he'd come home to find she'd piled his packed and travel-worn duffel bags outside their apartment door.

Then those envelopes had come back to him one too many times, and he'd finally given up sending them. Given up hope. Given up thoughts of ever seeing his son.

He shoved his hand into his back pocket again, grazing his wallet and running the details of the newspaper clipping inside it silently through his mind.

Scott Andrew Slater.

Born not to Layne McAndry but to Layne Marie Slater. She'd taken back her maiden name and put not one mention of his in the birth announcement. She had very likely wiped his memory from her mind.

Just as he'd forced himself to do to her for all these years.

JASON RAISED HIS fist in front of the apartment door, flinched as second thoughts hit him, and lowered his arm again.

Removing his Stetson, he scrubbed his forehead with one hand and assured himself he was doing the right thing. Close contact with two kids within two days last week had to mean something.

Yeah, something like fate deciding to rear up and head-butt him in the face, the way Burning Sage had almost done in that final ride in Cheyenne. The bull had wanted to take him down. Fate most likely just wanted to knock some sense into him.

Too late for that. He was here.

He raised his fist again and rapped on the apartment door. The wood sounded hollow, just the way his chest felt—if you didn't count his heart banging against his ribs.

Inside the apartment, a television's volume dipped, then a little boy's voice cried, "Mommy!" in stunned outrage. A second later, the doorknob rattled. The door swung open, and he stood staring at the girl he'd left behind.

The *wife* he'd left behind.

She looked like hell warmed over twice.

Her beautiful golden-brown hair had been pulled up and stuck every which way by a couple of plastic combs. Her skin was paler than he remembered, her nose glowed as red as the taillights on his truck, and her sky blue eyes looked as glassy and bloodshot as if she hadn't slept for a week.

Those eyes… In this situation, most folks' eyes would have widened in surprise. Instead, she blinked once and went blank-faced, the way she had always done when confronted with something that shocked or alarmed her. Right now, he imagined she had received a double dose of both.

"Jason?" Her voice came out in a croak. She reached up to rest her hand against the gaping neckline of her fuzzy blue robe.

The ragged tissue she held couldn't hide the sight of creamy skin patterned with a few small freckles. The vision did more for him than a slip-sliding blouse or skintight leather. It also triggered memories and feelings he forced himself to push aside. This conversation would be hard enough. He didn't need his body following suit. To combat the reaction, he took another deep breath and let it out. "Layne."

She covered a rattling cough with her forearm. "What do you want?"

Though he should have expected it, he was taken aback by the belligerent tone. He hadn't been ready for the question, either. Despite the long drive from Dallas, Texas, to Cowboy Creek, New Mexico, he hadn't prepared much for this meeting. Big mistake. He sure couldn't tell her he'd come back to make certain his son was in good hands. "I know it's been a while—"

"A while?" She coughed again, then shook her head, most likely in annoyance at him. "It's been almost four years since we've seen each other, and we've had no contact except filing for the divorce—"

"And—"

"—which made the split permanent."

"I know it did, but—"

"*Legally* permanent," she said heavily, leaning forward as if to emphasize her point.

He frowned.

She kept coming. The quick glance he caught of her suddenly greenish pallor clued him in. She was halfway to unconsciousness and ready to drop.

As he caught her to him, the door behind her swung open. A little boy stood just inside the frame. And somewhere in the apartment behind the kid, a baby let out an earsplitting screech.

LAYNE DID THE best she could with toothbrush and mouthwash and comb, but it wasn't much. And it was quick.

The symptoms she had been battling for two days now had gotten worse instead of better, and the short time on her feet showed her just how shaky this flu had left her. She gave thanks that when she had gone to answer the door, she hadn't been holding the baby.

The last thing she remembered before passing out was the look of alarm on Jason's face. When she had come to, she found herself cradled like a baby herself in his arms. She had fainted for only a second, he assured her. Still, ignoring her protests, he carried her into the small living room and deposited her on the couch.

Moments later, her stomach had heaved and she had bolted and here she was now, hiding in her bathroom the way she and her friends had hidden in the girls' room at school when they wanted to exchange gossip about the boys.

The only boy she'd ever had eyes for was Jason.

She heard her son's footsteps as he marched down

the hall. He came to a stop in the bathroom doorway. As awful as she felt, she couldn't help but smile at the sight of him. He and Jill were the lights of her life. Suddenly, he frowned, his eyebrows bunching together. She inhaled sharply, which led to another bout of coughing. Scott had her blue eyes and brown hair, but his frowning expression was pure Jason.

"Mommy sick?" he asked.

"Mommy's better," she said. She just didn't know how long that would last.

"I'm hungry."

The thought of food made her stomach quiver. "No problem, honey. How about—"

"Soup?"

She nodded. Luckily, she had made chicken soup a few weeks ago. The surplus she had stored in the freezer had gotten her through these past couple of days. She still had a large bowl of the soup in the refrigerator.

"Yes-s-s. *Es-s-s.* Soup for Scott for supper," he chanted in a singsong, laughing. He was learning the alphabet from his babysitter, who ran a day care from her house. To reinforce his lessons, here at home she played sound and word games with him. The sentence game was his favorite, and she had been so proud of him the day he'd created that sentence all by himself.

"Yes, soup for Scott for supper," she repeated in a singsong. "That sounds super, sweetie."

He laughed again. "That man will have soup, too?"

She froze. *No,* that man *will be long gone by suppertime.* "I'm not sure about that." She looked at the small clock she kept on the bathroom vanity and realized it was time to wake her daughter from her nap. "Come on, let's go get the baby and start that soup."

"Start soup for Scott for supper," he chanted, his voice fading as he went back down the hall toward the living room.

She tightened the long belt of her fuzzy robe and took one last look in the mirror. The teenage girl who had once fallen for Jason cringed and longed to reach for her makeup bag. But the woman she'd become lifted her chin and nodded at the reflection in the mirror.

Let him deal with her just the way she was now. It served him right for showing up unannounced after all this time.

She wasn't about to recall the way her heart had pounded and her head had swum and a tremor had run through her when she had opened the door to find him standing in the hallway. They were all simply reactions to the flu—and *anyone* could have passed out after getting hit with all those symptoms.

She also wasn't about to dwell on the past or worry about the intervening years or feel embarrassed by what had happened just a few minutes ago. She was going to get rid of Jason. Again. And hope this time he stayed gone.

As she turned to leave the bathroom, Scott began to yell. "Help! Help! You're not my daddy! Leave my sister alone!"

Every single word he screeched made her heart sink faster. She hurried down the hall and burst into the living room.

The baby lay in her playpen on the opposite side of the room, closer to the kitchen. Her beet-red face and gleaming eyes were sure signs she had woken up cranky and crying.

And, lost in thought, her mommy hadn't heard a peep.

Scott had taken a stance with his back to the playpen and his arms outstretched toward Jason as if holding a wild animal at bay. Jason stood a couple of feet from him, his hands patting the air presumably to calm her son.

Fighting another wave of dizziness, she put her hand on the door frame. "What's going on?" she demanded.

Chapter Two

Jason froze. Wasn't it bad enough to have the kid yelling and fending him off as if he were a tiger ready to pounce? He didn't need Layne standing there looking at him as if she considered him something much worse.

With a jerky movement, he showed her the yellow plastic pacifier he was holding. "I didn't know how long you'd be, and she looked like she was getting ready to start bawling up a storm again."

"Again?"

Confusion replaced her rebellious tone, making him swallow his irritation. She must not have recovered from her earlier fainting spell as completely as he'd thought she had. He nodded. "She was crying when I carried you in here and going even stronger when you bolted."

"Oh." Still looking shaky, she started across the room.

"Sit on the couch. I'll bring the baby to you."

When he moved forward, the boy tensed. "You're not my—"

"It's okay, Scott," Layne said quickly.

"But Miss Rhea says—"

"I know. But I'm right here, and I know this man."

Still eyeing him suspiciously, the kid stepped aside. "Okay. We can have soup now? I'm hungry."

The baby let out another screech. Jason put the pacifier in her mouth and bent over to lift her, supporting her head with one hand the way he'd seen Greg do with his daughter. Good thing he had. She couldn't have weighed much more than a kitten, but she was twice as wiggly and not nearly as cute with that red, wrinkled face. Sort of like her mama right now.

He'd think about that—and worry about whose kid she was—later. Layne looked ready to drop again, but if he didn't move soon, she would probably refuse to wait until he carried the baby over to her. He hurried across the room. "Sit," he said gruffly. "You don't want to take the chance of standing with her and passing out a second time, do you?"

She sank to the couch and took the baby from him. The girl immediately stopped crying and nuzzled the front of Layne's robe like a calf looking for her mama's milk.

"What's that about soup?" he asked.

"That's okay. I'll get it in a minute."

"Mommy, I'm *hung*-ry," the boy called. He still stood near the playpen as if he were afraid to get closer.

"You're not the only one, honey." The baby nuzzled again, and Layne raised her hand to her robe.

"Hey." He backed a step. "I'm just standing around taking up space. My cooking skills stretch as far as opening a can and putting a pot on the stove."

"Thanks," she said stiffly, "but we'll do just fine on our own. I hate to ask you to leave…"

I want you to go. Her eyes, looking like a couple of cold blue stones, got her point across as loud and clear and emphatically as her words had done a few years ago. Then, he had turned and walked out. Because he'd been a complete ass. Not without provocation, however. Seeing his packed bags at the front doorstep when he got home had warned him what to expect. Layne's response when he'd entered the apartment had underscored the message.

"*Mo*-mmy."

She looked past him to the boy and then back again. Now her gaze didn't quite meet his. "All right. The soup's not from a can. It's homemade. And the bowl is on the top shelf of the fridge." The baby let out a screech.

He half turned to the boy. "Come on, pardner, let's go get you some supper."

The boy looked at his mama, who offered him a nod of encouragement. Then he gave Jason a long, frowning look. "Okay," he said finally, his brow clearing. Getting that seal of approval made Jason stand taller. "Soup for Scott for supper."

"Yeah. Show me the way to the kitchen." The boy took off at a trot past the playpen. Jason's boots pounded against the bare flooring as he followed at almost the same speed. He sure didn't want to be around to watch Layne taking care of the baby.

Red nose, rumpled hair and bloodshot eyes aside, she was still the most beautiful girl he'd ever seen. Seeing any *more* of her as she opened her robe would only stir up memories best tucked away for good.

He found the soup where she'd directed and snagged a pot from the cabinet the boy pointed out to him.

"I help." His designated assistant…*his son* walked him through finding cups and bowls and spoons.

In amazement, Jason watched the little guy. Once that front door had opened, events had moved too rapidly for him to take everything in. Now the situation hit him and, for a minute, his legs threatened to go out from under him the way Layne's had.

Back in Dallas, his thoughts had been on making sure the boy was okay, that Layne was taking proper care of him and not just shutting him out of her life, shunting him to a sitter. And somewhere in the back of his mind, he'd convinced himself that having this confirmation would help make up for his own shortcomings.

Now he was home again and standing in an apartment not unlike the one he and Layne had shared when they got married. And he was getting supper ready… with his son.

His legs felt shaky again.

"I get napkins," the boy said.

"Sounds good."

He watched the child move around the room, seeming confident for a kid his age. That was the difference between being taught to be independent and having it forced on you, overwhelming you with the effort needed to survive. Assuming Layne had instilled that confidence in the boy, he gave her a lot of credit.

They set the table together. The room was filled with the sounds of spoons clanking against the table and the smell of chicken broth wafting from the pot on the stove. He wondered if someone had brought the soup over for Layne. Maybe she had made it herself. If so, she had turned into more of a homebody than she'd been when they had gotten married. Back then, they had stayed too busy in the bedroom to give her a chance to develop much skill in the kitchen.

Other memories he would do better to tuck away.

Scott stood looking at the almost neatly laid table.

He frowned. "We can eat supper on the couch? And watch TV?"

"I don't know about that. Your mama and your sister have taken over those seats right now." Recalling the words the boy had screeched at him made him wince. He knew the worries the kid would have, thanks to what Miss Rhea—whoever she was—had taught him. Understandably, he'd feel nervous, especially after watching a man he'd never before seen carry his mama into the apartment, and then seeing her run away. No wonder he was worried about that same man going near his baby sister.

Keeping an eye out for strangers had been one of the first things he'd learned as a child, and since then, the world had become a much scarier place. He didn't know how Layne took care of the kids by herself.

If she *was* on her own. There was the infant to account for, after all.

But if she had a man in her life, surely as sick as she was and with two babies to care for, the guy wouldn't have gone off and left—

He shoved the rest of the thought aside before it could take root in his mind.

What a jackass he'd once been. What a predicament he was in now.

This extended reunion had derailed his plan to take care of business and move on. Instead, he needed to take charge.

SHE HADN'T EXPECTED Jason to put on enough soup for all three of them, but he announced he had done exactly that. And when Scott came to take her hand to lead her to the kitchen, she couldn't say no. To tell the truth, with nothing in her stomach, she needed the nourishment, needed to get her strength back so she could take care of the kids and get Jason out of her life again.

Their awkward dinner would have taken place in near-silence if not for her son's chatter all through the meal and dessert.

She focused on getting her few spoonfuls of soup to her mouth without spilling anything…and on trying to keep her gaze on her soup bowl and away from her ex. And failing miserably. Every time he walked away from the table, she couldn't help sneaking a peek, couldn't help watching the way his muscles flexed beneath his gray T-shirt as he reached for dishes from the cabinet and the way his faded jeans pulled tight when he leaned down to pull the container of milk from the refrigerator.

When Scott had finished eating, Jason rose and began gathering up the dishes. He had taken control of her tiny kitchen and, worse, dominated her space. She was finding it hard to breathe, let alone keep her head upright. "Leave the dishes, please," she said. "I can take care of them."

"I don't think so."

He locked gazes with her. She managed to take a steadying breath and turn to Scott. "Honey, how about you go and get into your jammies for Mommy?"

"No, Mommy. I play with cars. *Please?*"

She smiled. "Well, we'll see. But jammies first. They're on your bed. You go get started, okay?"

He slid from his booster chair and left the room.

Slowly, she turned to face her ex-husband again. He had set the dishes in the sink. Hips settled back against the counter, he stood with his arms crossed and his biceps bulging against his T-shirt sleeves and his frown looking too much like Scott's for her liking. This situation was *all* too much for her and had been from the moment she had seen him standing in her hallway.

"Jason." Anger at him and irritation at herself made her hiss his name. "Just who do you think you are to tell me what I can and can't do in my own kitchen?"

"Just the guy who carried you back into the house after you passed out."

"It was only for a second. You told me that yourself."

"I lied."

Her breath caught. *"Why?"*

"The baby was wailing and the boy looked scared to death and you sure didn't seem in any shape for more bad news at that moment. The moment right before you ran off to toss your cookies. Remember that?"

"Yes," she snapped. She appreciated that he had been there at the time, but she didn't like having to feel grateful to him for anything. She didn't want to feel anything for him at all. "Then, thank you for carrying me in and taking care of supper. But I'm fine now. You can go."

He opened his arms wide, unknowingly allowing her a look at well-defined pecs and six-pack abs. He gestured around the room. "You're on the verge of collapse, and you expect me to leave you by yourself with two kids? What kind of man would that make me?"

"As far as I recall, the same kind who walked out when I was pregnant with *one* of those kids."

A muscle in his jaw worked hard, telling her he was having trouble holding back another response. The sight made her uneasy, not out of fear of him but from her memories of past fights. No matter how often they argued, he had almost always been better at hanging on to his anger than she had.

"You refused to talk to me," he said finally, his tone harsh but even. "And you kicked me out. Have you got a recollection of that day, too?"

"Yes," she snapped. "I remember it very well."

"Great. Then remember this, too. I didn't drop in only to say hello. I…I want to talk with you. But that can wait until you're feeling better again. I'll go. As soon as you call someone and they show up to stay with you." He crossed his arms again. "Dammit, Layne, you always were the most stubborn…"

It was his turn to take a deep breath. She bit her lip to keep from responding.

"Look," he continued, "you could barely handle the baby when she started squirming. And you were hanging on to the kitchen table with one hand while you stood up to strap her into her seat. You want to risk a serious accident while you're alone with the kids?"

She flushed. "Of course not."

"Then—"

"I don't have anyone to call."

"The baby's daddy—"

"He's not in the picture," she said shortly.

She could see him hesitate, as if her admission had thrown him. But he simply said, "What about your brother?"

"No. Cole's the best man in a wedding, and tonight's the rehearsal dinner. Everybody I know is involved one way or another in prepping for the wedding. Or they're working. That's where I would have been, too, if I hadn't called in sick."

"You have a job, along with taking care of two kids?"

She nodded. "I waitress at SugarPie's." She had started working at the small sandwich shop in the center of town after Jason had left. "Which means they're shorthanded without me there now, too."

"Well, that settles it." He returned to his seat across from her at the table and leaned forward until they were almost nose to nose. "You've got yourself an overnight guest."

"*No.* I'll find someone else to help me out." *Anyone else.* She shot to her feet to stare him down. The defiant movement did her in. Light-headed, she staggered, then struggled to regain her balance. The small amount of soup she had eaten churned in her stomach. With one hand over her mouth, she fled from the room.

Even as she hurried toward the bathroom, she frantically ran down a mental list of all her friends. Surely she could find one person who wasn't working and would come to her rescue.

Because Jason *couldn't* stay here all night.

LAYNE AWOKE WITH a start to find she still held the cordless phone. Frantically, she looked around the living room. The baby lay asleep in the playpen. Scott sprawled on the floor with his toy cars spread out around him.

Across from her, Jason sat in one of the overstuffed armchairs. He was flipping through a newspaper but looked up as soon as she shifted upright. "You went out like a TV with its plug yanked from the socket," he told her.

"Sorry." Her voice cracked. She prayed the dry spot in her throat wasn't the beginning of strep. The flu symptoms were enough to deal with. "How long was I asleep?"

"About an hour."

While he sat there and did her job, watching over her kids.

Sighing, she turned her attention to her son. "Bedtime, Scott."

He frowned. "No, Mommy. I play with cars. Look, my race cars." He pointed to a sheet of cardboard propped up by some of his plastic blocks that seemed to be serving as a motorway for his entire auto collection. At that moment, she didn't have the energy to argue, and an extra half hour or so of playtime wouldn't hurt him.

What hurt *her* was having to see Scott and his daddy together.

"Very nice," she managed. "Did you do that all by yourself?"

"No. Jason maked it."

"Oh." She looked at her ex. "Between getting supper and overseeing road construction, you seem to have *maked* yourself right at home."

"You'll thank me for that once I've gone and *maked* you a cup of tea for that throat."

He laughed, and the sound did things to her insides that had nothing to do with the flu. She crossed her arms over her chest, fighting a sudden shiver she couldn't blame on her illness, either. He frowned, and once again the resemblance to Scott made her breath catch. Over the years, she had tried not to notice the likenesses between her son and Jason. But seeing the two of them together only made the similarities between them undeniable.

Having the man right here in front of her only reinforced too many memories that had never completely faded.

"Have you got symptoms of anything else I should know about, besides flu?" he asked. "Judging by the way you crashed, I already suspect you've got sleeping sickness, too."

"Not that. At least, not yet. The only other thing I've got is called middle-of-the-night nursing fatigue. And of course, just generally being a mom." She swallowed, wincing at the dryness of her throat.

He rose. "I'll take care of that tea. How do you drink it?"

"Milk, no sugar," she said. As unhappy as accepting his offer made her feel, at this moment, she needed the warmth and comfort of the drink more than she needed control of the situation.

She ought to push him, to find out why he was here, to ask why he suddenly had something to say to her after all these years. At the reminder of his flat statement, uneasiness ran through her. But she just couldn't face interrogating him right now. Her head was swimming and her eyes felt watery, and the chills—a brand-new symptom—couldn't be a good sign at all, no matter whether they stemmed from her illness or her ex.

Jill continued to sleep peacefully and Scott sat engrossed in his car race. She took the opportunity to rest her eyes again until she heard the sound of the kettle whistling.

When Jason returned to the living room, he set two steaming mugs of tea on the coffee table.

"Jason, help," her son called. She looked in his direction and saw the cardboard raceway had slid from its supporting blocks and lay flat on the rug.

Jason went down on one knee beside Scott. Their matching expressions of concentration as they surveyed the fallen raceway shouted the fact they were father and son.

The observation made her throat tighten to the point of dry painfulness again. She grabbed the mug of tea. The warmth stung her mouth but soothed her throat and eased her chills. By the time Jason came back to take his seat, she had pulled herself together. Mostly.

"Any luck with your calls?"

She shook her head. Before falling asleep, she had contacted everyone she could think of who might be able to help her tonight. She was reluctant to admit defeat, but what else could she do? Besides, though she had heard dishes clattering and water running in the background while she made the calls, in this small apartment chances were good he had overheard almost all of her conversations.

"My options were limited," she confessed. "Most of the people I know are either attending the rehearsal dinner or involved in setting up for the wedding. Another few have plans for the night, and the rest have the flu bug themselves." She slumped back against the couch.

She would never admit it to him, but all the phone calls had worn her out. Of course, he had probably caught on to that by now, too. How could she have fallen asleep? She bit her lip and winced as the skin burned. Probably a sign of dehydration.

What else could go wrong tonight?

Jason stared at her over the rim of his tea mug. "I'm staying," he announced.

Chapter Three

The bull bearing down on him let out a bloodcurdling scream.

Jason jolted awake, jumped up from his seat in the armchair, cracked his shin against the coffee table and tripped over his boots, all at the speed of light. Another scream later, he made the connection between the onrushing bull and the baby down the hall.

He stumbled toward the bedroom Layne's kids shared. The glow of the night-light she had turned on showed him the way. But who needed a night-light when the high-pitched cries left no doubt about the right direction.

Scott lay curled up in a ball on the bed, apparently oblivious to the noise. His sister flailed her arms and legs and continued to scream, her face beet red in stark contrast to the pale yellow crib sheet.

He lifted the wriggling mass of baby. Afraid he would drop her, he brought her against his chest. She hiccupped a few times, then started rubbing her cheek against his shirt.

No way. He knew the game she wanted to play, and he didn't have the right equipment.

Reluctantly, he left the room and headed down the hall.

By now, he expected to see Layne coming to meet

him, but there was no sign of her. He frowned. Considering what he'd heard about most new mothers, she would have to be comatose not to respond to her baby's screams.

He hovered in the doorway of her room. When he'd announced he was staying, he had expected a scream from her, too, or at least a healthy protest. Her sighing acceptance and quick disappearance into her room after she'd put the kids to bed surprised him. They were also sure signs of how sick she must feel.

Her bedside clock read 2:38 a.m.

He hated having to wake her, but he had a hunch the baby's screams had halted only temporarily, and when they started up again, he would be in a worse predicament than he was now.

"Layne?" he said from the doorway.

She didn't move.

"Hey, Layne. The baby's hungry." And needing a change, judging by the warm weight of the pajama-clad bottom against his palm.

No sign of movement across the room. He went to the bed, then rested his hand on her shoulder and shook gently. "Hey, babe… *Layne.* Hey, Layne, wake up." Was that the sound of desperation in his voice? Over the suddenly renewed screams from the infant, he couldn't tell.

Now she stirred, rolling over onto her back. The pink sleep T-shirt she'd worn to bed twisted across her chest, leaving the deep neckline askew and barely covering her. He averted his gaze and tried to soothe the squirming baby, who had begun wriggling and twisting against *his* chest.

In desperation, he clicked on the bedside lamp. "Layne, wake up."

She blinked a few times. Squinting in the light, she shifted to a seated position and leaned against the headboard. She reached up to take the baby from him. "Oh-h-h," she cooed to the child, "somebody needs a change."

Her voice was low and sleep-sexy and made him think of things he needed, too. Another list of thoughts that were best forgotten. "How are you feeling?" he asked.

She didn't answer immediately, and he knew she didn't want to tell him the truth. "Awful," she said finally. She gestured toward the dresser. "Can you toss me that baby blanket, please? And there's a diaper bag on the shelf just inside the closet."

He handed her the lightweight blanket and found the bag.

"Normally," she murmured, her attention fixed on the baby, "I'm up and out of bed the second Jill lets out a cry. And now I didn't even hear her wake up."

"You've got reason."

Still looking away, she nodded. "I have to admit, I don't know what would have happened if you weren't here. Thank you."

"No problem." But there *was* a problem. What good was gratitude if she gave it grudgingly? If she couldn't even look him in the face?

She finished diapering Jill and cuddled the baby to her. In a low voice, she asked, "Why *are* you here?"

And there was another problem.

He had been about to lean against the edge of the dresser. Her question made him freeze. He still couldn't tell her the complete truth—not without the risk of having her kick him out again.

He told her a half-truth instead. "I wanted to see how things are going with you."

"Why?"

He shrugged. "Why not? We'd been together for—"

"Jason," she said quietly, "please don't try that one on me."

"All right, then. I wanted to see my son."

"*My* son," she corrected. "For all the contact you've had with him, you could have been a sperm donor."

JASON STOOD IN the doorway of the kids' room and watched his son rubbing the sleep from his eyes. Sitting in the middle of the double mattress, he looked so young and innocent. So small. Almost as small as the stuffed teddy bear and dilapidated panda taking up space on either side of him.

A minute ago, he had heard Scott calling for him and come at a run, hoping to keep the boy's cries from wakening the baby and, in turn, the baby from wakening Layne. Considering the occasional sounds of Layne's bedsprings creaking and, once, of her footsteps padding to the bathroom and back in the early hours, it had taken her till daybreak to get to sleep again.

"Morning now?" Scott asked.

"Yeah," Jason confirmed.

This morning had come fast and furiously for him, with no sleep at all once he had left Layne's room.

Furious couldn't begin to describe his reaction to her verbal slam. *Sperm donor.* A helluva thing to say to a man. Even if there *had* been one grain of truth in it, she had no call to dump the full silo load of responsibility on him. He wasn't the only one involved in how things had turned out.

He reached for the teddy bear for something to occupy his mind and hands. The bear looked well loved, with its fur matted in some places and its cloth body worn bare in others. Had Scott gotten the bear as a birthday gift? Had he slept with it ever since? Did he like it better than the panda he had just grabbed from the bed?

"Have to hug Teddy," Scott said.

"What?"

"Morning now. Have to hug Teddy," Scott said again. He wrapped his arms around the panda hard enough to squeeze the stuffing from it. "See?"

Jason froze. He was a rodeo rider and a hard-riding wrangler, and he didn't hug anything that wasn't female and wearing a dress and willing to hug him back. He didn't do stuffed animals.

"Have to hug Teddy," Scott said yet again.

He could hear the slight tremor in the boy's voice and see his puzzled frown. Evidently, Layne had made those early-morning hugs a family tradition. He swallowed hard, trying to ease the lump in his throat. "Yeah," he mumbled. "Hug Teddy." Feeling like a fool, he wrapped his arms around the little cloth body. Feeling worse, he watched the smile brighten his son's face and wished he could hug his boy instead.

How many mornings like this had he missed over the years? He didn't want to think about it, refused to count the days. There would be too many for him to handle and way too many for him ever to replace.

Scott glanced toward the crib. Jason looked in that direction, too, and saw Jill staring wide-eyed at the mobile of puppies and kittens hanging at one end of the crib. Could babies her age even see that far? She looked only a few weeks old.

Scott threw aside his covers and crawled to the edge of the bed. "Morning now. Mommy says time to do the diaper. *De-e-e*," he said in a singsong. "Time to do the diaper."

Jason frowned, knowing he'd have to draw the line there. He'd just mastered the task of tucking Jill into her crib without waking her, and even that had about taxed his skill.

But Scott padded over to the small white dresser and pulled a diaper from the bottom drawer. He returned to stand in front of Jason with the diaper held out toward him and with the same expression of expectancy as when he had wanted him to hug the bear. A look of complete trust.

He suddenly wished Layne would look at him that way.

Even better at the moment, he wished Layne would wake up and walk into the room.

"I'm green at this, pardner," he admitted, taking the diaper.

"Green?" Scott said, looking at him with his mouth open, probably expecting to see him turn into an alien before his very eyes.

"A greenhorn," he explained, feeling foolish again. How could he explain that concept to a three-year-old? How could he explain anything when he'd never had the practice? The chance? All he could do was try. "It means I'm new at this. A beginner. Someone who's just learning."

"I learn my ABC's!" Scott grinned.

He smiled back at him. "Yeah, that's it. Just like you learn your ABC's. I'm a greenhorn at doing diapers."

"De-e-e," the boy chanted again. "Greenhorn at doing diapers."

This time, Jason laughed aloud and ruffled the boy's hair.

Why couldn't *he* be such a quick study?

It was a sobering idea. Especially when he connected the thought to getting what he wanted from Layne.

In the years he'd been gone, once he'd stopped sending her those envelopes she kept returning, he'd given up worrying about her. She was an adult. She could take care of herself—as she had made all too plain to him. No doubt about it, the woman had a way with words.

But the boy...

When he'd left, the child hadn't been close to being born yet, hadn't even made his appearance evident in the swelling of Layne's belly. Hadn't, somehow, been real to him. Now, his son was very real, as smart as a whip and as loving as his mama. A little boy his daddy could be—and *was*—proud to know was his.

But could he be the kind of man, the kind of daddy, to make his little boy proud of him?

For the tenth time already that morning, Layne sighed. Her comment to Jason last night about being her son's sperm donor had been cruel—and yet it certainly had been truthful. In any case, Jill's fresh cries to be fed had saved her from having to hear his response. He had left the room at a speed she would have found laughable... if not for the thoughts that assailed her as she watched him walk out the door.

He had taken one look at her getting ready to nurse and had bolted, just as he'd done in the living room earlier. The sight made her think of so many *shoulds*, her heart hurt. Instead of running, he should have felt comfortable watching her feed the baby. He should have had that experience with Scott. He should have been in the delivery room the day their son was born.

The one thing he never should have done was leave.

After she had finished nursing, returned the baby to her crib and staggered blurry-eyed back to her own bed, it had taken her almost till dawn before she was finally able to fall into an exhausted sleep. She felt grateful it let her forget the memories. At least, until she had woken up to find them at the front and center of her mind again.

As she dressed, she left a terse message on a friend's cell phone. She hated to call Shay O'Neill. Though they hadn't been in many of the same classes all through school, they had gotten closer during the past year or so. Shay worked just down the street from SugarPie's at Cowboy Creek's ice cream parlor, the Big Dipper. After she closed up the shop, she would often stop in at SugarPie's. On a quiet night, the two of them would spend some time chatting. Right now, Shay had enough on her mind. But Layne desperately needed some help to send Jason on his way.

In the kids' room, she found both the bed and the crib empty. As she went down the hall toward the kitchen, she heard Scott's voice raised in question and the deep rumble of Jason's reply. The sound of his voice made her chest hurt.

Yesterday, her first sight of him standing in the hall had stolen her breath. He looked good, so good. Better than she ever remembered him looking, from the day he had first walked into her classroom in grade school. Even then he had been gorgeous, and with that one glance at him, her fate had been sealed.

Seeing him so unexpectedly last night had shaken her. She couldn't deny it.

But she couldn't do anything about any of this now except send the sights and thoughts and feelings and memories—and her oh-so-sexy-looking ex—back to the past where they all belonged.

In the kitchen, Jill lay in her carrier on the table. Scott knelt on a chair, his attention focused on one of his coloring books.

Frying bacon scented the air, and a bowl of beaten eggs sat on the counter. Jason stood at the stove. He wore a snug blue T-shirt and had tucked a red-checkered hand towel into the waist of his jeans. His dark hair waved and tumbled, free-falling in the way that had always made her breath catch to see it. After they made love, he would comb his fingers through the strands to tame them, then laugh as she rumpled them again.

He eyed her from across the room. A familiar stubble darkened his jawline. The set of that jaw told her he wasn't completely overjoyed to see her.

He gave her a tight smile. "You're just in time for breakfast."

Thank goodness, her stomach didn't roil at his words. She nodded and took her seat at the table.

Also thank goodness, having both Jill and Scott in the room would keep Jason from following the conversational path he had attempted to lead her down the night before. It was pointless for him to tell her why he was here. It was just as senseless for her to obsess about *shoulds*. There was nothing between them, and the sooner she saw the last of him, the better.

"I'll have these done in just a minute." He beat the

eggs and poured them into her largest frying pan with a practiced ease that surprised her.

"When did you learn to cook?" she asked.

He laughed. "I might say the same about you if you made that soup from scratch." He eyed her questioningly, and she nodded. "Not bad. But neither of us was too handy in the kitchen a while back, were we? I learned out of necessity since I have to take a turn in the bunkhouse. I'm still not so hot at it, so the boys let me get away with handling only breakfast. But I do a darned good omelette." He stirred the eggs in the pan, then looked sideways at her. "How are you feeling?"

"Better. *Much* better."

"You didn't get a lot of sleep."

"Enough. Believe me, lately, a two-hour stretch is a marathon." She eyed Jill's fresh jumper and noted the lumpiness of the diaper beneath it. Jason must have made an effort. Tears rose to her eyes. She blinked them away. "You changed the baby?"

"Me and Jason did," Scott said. "*De-e-e*. Greenhorn at doing diapers."

Last night, she had noticed how quickly her ex had gone from *that man* to *Jason*. This phrase was also a new one for her son—and for her. She stared at him, then glanced at Jason. "'Greenhorn at doing diapers?'" she repeated.

"It's a guy thing."

"Right." She turned back to Scott. "Oh, dear—a dirty diaper?"

"A danged dirty diaper," Jason said.

Scott laughed till he almost toppled off the chair. She wondered if he had told Jason about their game.

"I don't imagine you'll be up for doing a lot yet."

She stiffened. He couldn't insist on staying here all day. Or could he? He'd been adamant enough last night. "I'll be fine. I told you, I'm feeling much better. And a friend of mine is stopping by this morning." Shay would listen to the phone message she had left and would pick up on the tension in her voice. She wouldn't let her down.

Not the way Jason had.

He transferred the bacon to a paper-towel-lined platter. "Between being sick and having no one to watch the kids, seems like you're going to have to miss the wedding," he said. "Who's getting married, anyhow?"

"Pete Brannigan."

"You're kidding. Thought he'd already gone down that road before we...before."

"He did. He's going down that road again." Just the way she had. Unlike her, Pete had made a much better choice his second time around. "He's Jed Garland's ranch manager now, and he's marrying one of Jed's granddaughters."

She touched Jill's tiny fist. "Pete has two young kids of his own. He and Jane will understand that I can't make it." She gave a half laugh. "It's Jed who will be upset if everyone in town doesn't show up for the ceremony and the reception afterward. He and his family reopened the banquet room at the Hitching Post. They've started holding weddings there again, too. He's so happy all three of his granddaughters are walking down the aisle right there on Garland Ranch. Well, one already has. Jane will be the second."

"Too bad they weren't back in the wedding business when we got married."

She looked at him in surprise. "We couldn't have afforded a reception there—or anywhere else, for that matter. We were lucky to have rings and enough left over for me to buy a dress." *Lucky.* Or so she had thought.

She stared down at the tabletop.

At the time, she had been so in love with Jason, she would have worn ragged jeans and flashed a beer can pop-top for her wedding ring.

Despite everything, she couldn't regret that ceremony. Her marriage had given her Scott, and she could never wish away her son or her daughter.

Still, she should have known better than to marry her high-school sweetheart. She should have waited till the heat of the moment—the heat of their relationship—had burned itself out, as it had always been bound to do.

Speaking of burning...

She caught the distinct scent of breadcrumbs beginning to char. Rising, she said, "I'd better grab the toast. That old thing's getting temperamental." She popped the lever of the toaster and removed the slices to a plate.

This far from the table, she could talk to Jason without Scott overhearing. "Thanks for starting breakfast," she said in a low voice. "I'll take over from here. I don't want to hold you up, and I'm sure you'd much rather eat in peace and quiet at SugarPie's."

He frowned. "I'm willing—"

"Thanks," she repeated firmly. "I appreciate all you've done, but I'm fine now. Really. A few solid hours of sleep were all I needed. And I won't be alone. I told you, I have a friend dropping by."

She had called Shay deliberately to give herself an out this morning. Maybe it was the coward's way out. She couldn't help that now.

Ordinarily, she would stand up for herself and her kids and send Jason packing. But somehow, she couldn't seem to gather the strength to do that. Or to face another argument with him and all the memories that would surface along with it.

The flu, of course. No matter how much better she felt this morning, she wasn't quite herself yet, and she could—and *did*—blame her weakness solely on the flu bug.

"So," she continued, "you'll be able to go on your way."

As if on cue, the doorbell rang.

She swallowed a sigh of relief and plucked the spatula from his hand. "Since you're so willing to help, you *can* do me one last favor, please. Answer the door."

Chapter Four

At the Hitching Post Hotel, Jason paced from the long, waist-high reception desk, across the lobby to the wide doorway of the sitting room opposite, and back again. On his drive to the hotel, he had fought a mix of anger and irritation that had gotten stronger by the mile. Now he'd arrived, he wasn't sure what had brought him here, except the determination not to leave town yet. Not to let Layne have the last word—again.

"That's new flooring," a familiar voice drawled from behind him. "It'd be a shame to wear grooves into it this soon."

Jason turned to face the tall white-haired man now standing alongside the reception desk. He returned the familiar smile. Jed Garland had once been like a father to him.

Jason nearly staggered from the slap on his shoulder the older man gave him and found his hand engulfed in Jed's.

"It's been quite some time, boy. I thought maybe we'd never see you back on this ranch again. You looking for work?"

He shook his head. "No. I'm here for a place to stay."

Jed raised his white eyebrows. "How long are you planning to stick around?"

"I don't know." He shrugged. "It's complicated."

"Life can be. All we can do is our best."

"Yeah." Lately it seemed he'd fallen down in that regard a long time ago. At Jed's level stare, tension tightened his belly. Who knew what Layne had told folks about their split and his disappearance. The memory of the comment she'd slammed him with last night—about his contribution to their son's birth—kicked up his tension a notch.

Damn, she didn't pull any punches. She never had. The worst of it was, he deserved the hit.

"Follow me." Jed led the way toward the doorway behind the registration desk. "We'll take over Tina's office and sit for a while. The girls are all getting ready to head to town to prepare for Jane's big day tomorrow."

As Jed closed the door behind them, Jason took a seat in the guest chair, leaving the one behind the desk for Jed. "I hear Pete and Jane are tying the knot. *And* that you had a hand in roping them together."

The older man laughed. "They are, and I did. This is wedding number two, and the third one won't be too far along the road."

"I'll have to track down Pete and say hello." The two of them had once worked together as wranglers, being broken in while under Jed's supervision.

"He'll appreciate seeing you, I'm sure." Jed leaned back in the swivel chair with his hands linked behind his head. "I didn't realize you'd kept up with the goings-on in Cowboy Creek after you left town."

"I...saw Layne. She filled me in on everything."

"I also didn't realize you two kept in touch."

He didn't fall for Jed's apparent innocence. The man had always had his ways of finding out anything that went on in Cowboy Creek, and everyone understood if there was one thing Jed Garland was famous for, it was *knowing*. It wouldn't have come as a surprise to learn Jed had already heard about his arrival in town yesterday. "We don't keep in touch. We hadn't even spoken to each other in years until last night."

"Another of life's complications, huh? You and Layne seemed to deal with more of those than most kids."

He'd always felt comfortable talking with Jed back in those days. The man had been good at keeping confidences to himself, and Jason would risk betting that was still true. "I spent the night at her place," he said. "She wasn't feeling well and needed somebody to help her out."

"That was nice of you."

"Yeah." So anyone would think. Except Layne. He'd done his best to care for her and the baby and their son. And what had that gotten him? A sucker punch that had nearly knocked him to his knees.

My son, she had stressed last night. She had been as quick to draw the line about that as she had in throwing her verbal right hook about his lack of involvement with Scott. Knowing she was right hadn't made him feel any better. "It was just to help her out for the night," he clarified. "And now, I'm looking for a room."

"So you said. Well, we're nearly full up with everyone here for the wedding. But we'll fit you in…somehow. You also said Layne's sick, though, didn't you? Has she got the flu that's going around?"

"Yeah. But she said she was feeling better this morning." The minute she had claimed that, the second she'd found someone else to help her, she had tossed him out.

"From what I hear, folks don't recover too quickly from it." Jed's piercing blue gaze made him want to break off eye contact, but he managed to hold the man's gaze. "And you just went off and left her?"

"No. Shay O'Neill's with her. I thought you could pass along the word to her brother that she could use a hand."

Jed shook his head. "Cole won't be around. He and the other groomsmen are off to Santa Fe with Pete, helping him get through his last day as an unmarried man."

Jason tried to hide his grimace. "I wouldn't think there'd be any 'getting through' about it. Being unmarried's a good thing."

"Not always. Not when you're a single parent like Pete. Or like Layne."

"Jed—" He clamped his jaw tight.

The other man nodded. "Good choice. There's no sense trying to argue your way out of that one when you haven't been around to see what's going on. Now, you know darned well that whenever we talked in the past, I never pulled any punches with you. And I'm not about to start. I never steered you wrong, either, so I'll tell you this flat-out straight. Cole's not here to look in on his sister and the kids. My girls have their day planned, too. And I happen to know Shay's joining them all for lunch at SugarPie's."

Jed rose from his seat. Automatically, Jason stood, too. "I'll hold a room for you, no worries there, but if I were you, I'd seriously consider hightailing it back to Layne's and seeing what else you can manage to help her out with. It's the only decent thing to do."

He nodded. He recognized Jed's thinly veiled attempt

to shame him into doing what the man wanted. An easy agreement to the suggestion might have looked like he was giving in. But so what? He'd already come to the same conclusion himself.

Even as he'd driven away in the white heat of anger, he had known he wasn't going for long. He had to see Layne, because his plans had changed. His intention had been to get her to take the child support she had always refused to accept. But after seeing the boy—after spending time with his son—after connecting with Scott the way he had done that morning, no matter how brief the link might have been, the situation had changed. Now he wanted more.

For his son's sake and his own, he wanted contact with his child.

"WHAT ARE YOU up to, Abuelo?"

At the sound of his youngest granddaughter's voice, Jed Garland started. He pushed aside his coffee mug on the Hitching Post's kitchen table and glanced at Tina. "What makes you think I'm up to anything?"

Grinning, she took a seat. "The last time you had that look on your face, you were plotting how to get Mitch and Andi together. So I'll ask again, just what are you up to?"

He grinned back. He loved all his granddaughters equally, but Tina had grown up in this very hotel and they knew each other best—which, come to think of it, didn't always work to his advantage. But today he definitely saw the benefits to their relationship. "While you girls were all upstairs, I had a visitor. A new hotel guest, actually, and you'll never guess who."

"So tell me."

"Jason McAndry."

Tina's breath hitched. "You're kidding. What is he doing home?"

"Seeing Layne, for one thing. When he stopped in, he'd just come from her apartment."

"Have you told Cole?" Coincidentally, Cole was both Layne's brother and Tina's husband.

"No, I haven't, and for now, I think that's something we'll need to play close to our vests. If Cole hears Jason's back in town, it'll ruin all my plans."

"Plans? You mean…? You're not thinking about Layne and Jason as a couple, are you?" She shook her head. "You're a wonderful matchmaker, Abuelo, but there's no chance you'll get those two back together."

He frowned. "You're a fine one to say that, after the state you and Cole were in not so long ago."

"That was different. Layne and Jason have already been married. And divorced."

"And you think as a wonderful matchmaker, I haven't already considered that?" He reached across the table to pat the back of her hand. "Haven't you learned a lot yourself about the redeeming power of love?"

"Yes, I have," she said softly, "thanks to a little help from my own private matchmaker."

"Then trust your old grandpa, won't you, and return the favor. I want to keep Cole from finding out for a bit. Give these kids a chance for more time on their own."

"But you said Jason planned to stay here. He and Cole will see each other at breakfast tomorrow."

"No, I don't believe they will. When Jason left again this afternoon, he was headed back to Layne's…thanks to a little nudging, I might add. He'd already spent the night with her." Tina's jaw dropped, and he laughed.

"Not what you're thinking, girl. I played dumb with Jason, but you and I both know Layne's down with the flu. He kept an eye on the kids for her so she could catch up on her sleep. Now I've got him back there, I need to *keep* him there. I can't get you involved, at least not just yet."

"That's true. Not if you plan to leave Cole out of the loop."

"And I surely do. We need to get someone else to pull the strings for a bit, while we stay in the background. Someone to be our eyes and ears, at least, and keep us *in* the loop."

"You mean someone to spy for us, don't you?"

He chuckled and repeated, "I surely do. I've got lots of folks who can do that from a short distance. But we need someone who can get close to Layne. Who's our best bet?"

"Well...considering Layne goes in to work at Sugar-Pie's every day, I would say Sugar, of course."

"No, thank you. That woman would want to run the whole show."

She laughed. "Like someone else I know." She thought for a moment. "One or two of the other waitresses might do, but I think Layne's closer to Shay O'Neill."

"Yes." He slapped his hand on the table. "Shay would be downright perfect. In fact, Jason said she's over with Layne right now. Give her a call and tell her we need to speak with her."

"I'll be seeing her in town—"

"Even so. Let her know to be careful what she says around Layne—and the other girls—before we get a chance to sit down with her. And when you all are done with your shopping, make sure to get her out here to see us."

"To get her on our side, you mean."

"That's my girl." He grinned. "I do believe you're catching on to this matchmaking business."

"ARE YOU SURE you're going to be okay on your own with the kids?"

Layne looked at Shay's worried frown and managed to nod. "I'll be fine." But, despite the afghan tucked around her and the cup of tea in her hands, she shivered. Chills from the flu had combined with what she suspected was a delayed reaction to seeing Jason again.

She couldn't have felt more relieved—or more guilty—when Shay had walked in the door and he walked out. "I shouldn't have called you—"

"Of course, you should have. I'm your friend."

"I know, but you're busy with work and helping out with the wedding. And with so many other things." Shay's grandmother, Maureen, was getting up in age, and Shay did a lot for her. "How's Mo?"

"Good days and bad."

"And how are *you* feeling?"

"Fine."

Shay was pregnant and due in the near future. She would talk about her pregnancy, about her excitement at becoming a mom. But Layne knew better than to mention anything about the dad. Months ago, Shay had confided his name to Layne but sworn her to secrecy. At the same time she had made it clear he wouldn't be a part of her life.

Shay tucked a strand of her long blond hair behind her ear and glanced down at her rounded stomach. "I'm getting bigger every time I take a peek." She eyed Layne again. "And you're not getting away with changing the subject."

"I wasn't trying to. I was just pointing out that you have a lot on your mind."

"So do you." Shay added quietly, "It's not every day an ex-husband shows up and spends the night." From the purse she had set on the coffee table, her cell phone rang. "Sorry, I have to grab this. I'm on call for some extra hours at the Big Dipper, and I sure could use them... Hello?"

Layne tuned out Shay's voice but couldn't stop thinking of what she had just said.

It's not every day an ex-husband shows up and spends the night.

Hearing that, Layne had had to swallow a groan. The truth was, she already had not *an* ex-husband but *two* ex-husbands to her credit. Or more like it, discredit. Either way, she certainly had no luck when it came to men.

Shay ended her call and dropped the cell phone back into her bag. "I'm sorry again, Layne. I wish I could offer to take care of the kids for the rest of the day." She grinned. "I need all the practice I can get. But that was Tina. The bridal party's meeting for lunch at SugarPie's and then doing some shopping, and they had invited me along. She was letting me know they're already here in town. I could cancel—"

"No, you couldn't. Go and have fun. I told you, I'll be fine."

Shay smiled. "Maybe you can get Jason to come back. And to stay over again."

Layne sighed. "He didn't 'stay over.' At least, not in

the way you probably meant when you said he'd spent the night."

"Maybe you wish he had?"

"No."

From her playpen a few feet away, Jill let out a surprised squawk.

Layne lowered her voice again. "I don't want anything to do with Jason. And I wouldn't have called you, but I just couldn't think of any other graceful way to get him to leave."

"Why would you want to? It's been years since the two of you were together. People change." She hesitated. "Well, *some* people. Maybe you and Jason both have. And obviously, he cares about you and the kids, or he wouldn't have volunteered to stay here to take care of them."

She flushed, thinking of her comment to him last night, her remark about his lack of involvement with their baby. She certainly hadn't worried about being graceful then.

"I'm not trying to pry," Shay said, "and I know you don't like to talk about him. And you know just how well I relate to that. But I have to say, in school you two seemed like the perfect couple."

"We were. When we were between arguments."

"Really?"

She nodded. Last night, she wouldn't have made that comment to him at all if she hadn't already had a headful of memories of those battles.

She wanted to continue to keep conversations about him off-limits, but his reappearance in her life made that impossible. She needed to talk to someone. And she did trust Shay. "We were teenagers," she said finally. "You know how that goes. Our relationship bounced all along the emotional spectrum. Hot-and-heavy romance at one end and cold-war fights at the other."

"And kissing and making up in the middle?"

She laughed bitterly. "Yes. Along with one especially long stretch of peace that got us in front of a judge and put a wedding ring on my hand. But the peace treaty didn't hold up." She shrugged. "It was just as well. Things wouldn't have worked out for us anyway."

Considering they lived in a constant state of high emotions, even if they had managed to avoid their final argument, the one that led to her kicking him out, their relationship never would have lasted. She had told him she had reached her limit—he had left her at home alone just one too many times.

What she hadn't told him was the reaction his absence always triggered inside her, the sense of abandonment she felt. She could handle that...until they had a baby on the way. If he couldn't manage to stay home at night when it was just the two of them, how would he handle being a new daddy with a crying infant?

"Maybe the two of you ought to give things another try," Shay said.

"No, thank you. I'm just glad I managed to get him out of my life again this morning." As she plopped her teacup down on the coffee table for emphasis, a knock rattled the apartment door. A rhythmic quick-tap she had long ago learned to recognize as Jason's.

The few times he'd come to her house to meet her, she had loved hearing that special signal just for her. Now, it only made her groan and slump against the couch.

"What's the matter?" Shay asked. "Are you okay?"

"You won't believe me when I tell you. I'm fine, but I

need you to run interference with Jason for me again." At the confusion on the other woman's face, she laughed—though there was nothing at all funny about the situation. "I recognize the sound of his knock on the door."

Chapter Five

When the door closed behind Shay, Jason dropped into the armchair he'd begun to think of as his. A dangerous thought, and a useless one. He wouldn't be in town long enough to get attached. If Layne had her way, he suspected he wouldn't be around here long enough to keep the seat warm.

Already he could see her building up steam to blast him in irritation. She'd held back with Shay here, but now she had nothing stopping her. Before she could start in again, he held up his hand. "Look. We've been through this already—last night and again just now with Shay. You've got no one else to call. She said she won't be able to stop by again at all today and probably not all weekend, especially with the wedding tomorrow. And you saw how much of a hurry she was in to leave."

"Because you bullied her."

He snorted. "I said, 'Fancy meeting you here again.' She laughed. Then, after delivering the news about her schedule, she was out the door before you or I could open our mouths. Obviously she's busy. I've got nothing on my plate at the moment. And now I'm back here, I'm not going anywhere."

"Jason!" Scott called. "Play cars today?"

He shot a glance at the boy. "Yeah," he said firmly. "We'll play cars while your mama takes a nap." He looked back at Layne. His voice pitched lower, he added, "You've had your fun tossing me out. Not once, but twice. Do you really need to ram your point home by going for a third try?"

She glared at him and clutched the afghan more closely around her, but she kept her voice down. "After the way you barged in here, is there any reason I shouldn't tell you to go?"

"I guess not. You'd never needed much of an excuse before."

She gasped. "If you're talking about what happened years ago, you're way out of line. You gave me plenty of reasons back then. And once you'd walked away to go who knows where to spend the night with who knows what little—"

"Layne," he snapped.

Visibly, she struggled to take a breath. "And then the next morning—what? You assumed I would be overjoyed you decided to come back? You never told me what made you think that—"

"You never gave me a chance," he began, but she was on a tear, her voice rising with every word.

"—you just assumed you could walk right in and find your way to my bed again. I wasn't—"

"*Our* bed. And you weren't having any of that. Yeah, I know. You made your feelings perfectly clear." Swallowing hard, he looked away for a long moment, watching Scott with his toys. Regardless of what he could have said back then to defend himself, it wouldn't have mattered. The marriage was over anyway. It had been long past time for him to leave.

But now, his son mattered. His son was his purpose for coming back and the only reason he was here in this room at this moment. Layne's illness simply gave him the excuse to hang around.

"That's all in the past," he said. "History. I'm not trying to find my way anywhere near you now. I only want to help, and only because you're not feeling well." Even as she shook her head, her eyes gleamed from the fever she wouldn't admit to having. "No sense denying it. It's obvious. It's also plain to see I'm the last person you want here. Earlier this morning, you couldn't wait to get me out of the house."

"But I didn't toss you out."

He shrugged. "All right, let's just say you worked danged hard to find a replacement for me. But now Shay's gone—taking away your last option—and you don't have a choice." He sure wasn't going to let anyone blame him for an emergency he could have prevented. "One weak moment while you're holding the baby... one second of fade-out when Scott's near the stove... anything can happen. Let's face it, you don't want me here, but I'm all you've got to give you a hand with the kids."

As if on cue, the baby let out a screech. Layne tossed off the afghan and attempted to stand. Her legs looked about as strong as a minute-old calf's.

"I'll get her," he said, rising to his feet.

Gotta hand it to kids for creating a good diversion.

When he placed the baby into Layne's arms, she nodded and mumbled a grudging thanks.

"Do you need anything?" he asked.

"A fresh cloth. There's a folded stack in my closet, right beside where you'd gotten the diaper bag."

"Be right back." He headed out of the room, shaking his head.

Scream fests and sex.

That had been the story between the two of them after they'd married, although his teenage hormones sure hadn't found it a problem back then. They would both get all hot under the collar, usually over the stupidest things and always at the wrong times. They liked to fight. And they liked the makeup sex even better.

The thought of those times left him all thumbs. When he reached into her closet for a cloth, he fumbled and toppled the stack. The cloths knocked over the diaper bag, which fell against a small cardboard box, which went tumbling from the shelf. Reflexes kicked in, allowing him to grab the box before it hit the floor. But the lid fell off midgrab and the box, upended, spilled its contents across the carpet.

Biting back a curse, he knelt to scoop up the papers.

And the cards.

And the photos.

A lump lodged in the back of his throat, making it hard for him to breathe and impossible for him to swallow. Looked like she had saved every danged card and love note he'd ever given her and every photo they'd ever taken together.

He froze with his hand hovering over a shot he remembered all too well, a picture of Layne sitting on his lap in a pink-cushioned chair at SugarPie's. Sugar always kept a camera on hand in the sandwich shop. She had snapped the shot of them just after they had told her they were gonna be a mama and daddy.

Slowly, he picked up the photo. He had wrapped his arms around Layne and rested his cheek against her soft hair. Her eyes glowed, and her smile stretched as wide as he'd ever seen it. They were barely out of the newly-wed stage and deliriously happy at their news. And so appallingly young to have a baby on the way.

Hurrying, he crouched to sweep up everything that had spilled onto the carpet, then shoved it all back into the box. He slammed the lid in place and returned the box to the shelf. Not one of those actions could help him forget anything he had seen or felt or thought. But they all went a long way toward reinforcing what he finally had to admit.

He groaned, recalling that day at SugarPie's and feeling a certainty at this moment he hadn't realized back then. A certainty he didn't want to think about now.

He and Layne never should have gotten married in the first place.

THAT EVENING, JED and Tina finally managed to find a quiet place to chat with Shay. Tina had taken her upstairs to the suite the girls had been using for their wedding preparations. Once the coast was clear downstairs, he moseyed on up to join them.

They were both working on the party favors for tomorrow's wedding, tying ribbons around small crystal vases filled with foil-wrapped chocolates.

The minute he brought up Jason and Layne, he knew he and Tina wouldn't have a problem winning Shay over to their side. As soon as he mentioned the pair, she was with him, confirming his impression those two weren't as uninterested in each other as they'd tried to let on.

"I suggested she might have liked having Jason there for the night, and she jumped all over me," Shay admitted.

"Protesting too much?" he asked.

She nodded. "That's just what I thought. I tried to tell her he could really care about her and the kids, and the idea made her turn ten shades of red. And you should have seen the look on her face when he came back to the apartment."

"She wasn't expecting him again?" Tina asked.

Shay shook her head. "I don't want to break any confidences…"

"And we don't want you to," he assured her. He liked her loyalty. He liked the girl herself. As well as being his old friend Mo's granddaughter, Shay was a valued employee of the Hitching Post and a good friend to Layne. And to all of the Garlands. She deserved happiness as much as his girls did. One day, he'd have to do something about that.

He smiled encouragingly at her. "Just give us the gist so we know we're on the right track."

"Well, she tells me she doesn't want anything to do with Jason, and I… I can understand that. And this morning she tried to put on a good front with me, but I could tell she wasn't happy he had left the apartment earlier. Then he came back again right after Tina called me, just before I was leaving. And the look on her face— and on his, come to think of it…"

"There's more going on than they want people to think?" Tina asked.

"I don't know…" Shay considered a moment. "I'm not sure anything's going on yet. And I wouldn't even be telling you all this, except I get the feeling they wouldn't be opposed to something happening. And the funny thing is, I don't think either one of them is aware of it themselves."

Jed grinned. "Now, you see," he said to Tina, "this is just what I was talking about. Shay was on hand to get the lay of the land, so to speak."

"What do you want me to do?" Shay asked.

"Nothing, for the moment. I've got Jason half-convinced nobody from the ranch has time to look in on Layne. I don't think he'll be going anywhere, at least for the next day or two. And you'll be busy with the wedding tomorrow anyway. For now, let's give 'em this time together, and then after the weekend, we'll have you take another reading."

The two girls exchanged a look.

"What about Cole?" Tina asked.

"Same thing," he said promptly. "Nothing for the moment. Tonight, by the time the boys all get back from living it up in Santa Fe, I imagine they won't have much on their minds but rolling into bed and sleeping off the effects of having a good time."

"What happens if Layne starts feeling better?" Tina asked. She turned to Shay. "She might be having mixed feelings about Jason, but she's also got strong feelings about being independent. I know it frustrates Cole that she won't take more help from him."

"I know what you mean, and I agree," Shay said. "I can't see her letting Jason stay there once she's well enough to handle things on her own."

He nodded. "Even if she does want the boy around, she'll tell him to go, just to save face."

"Exactly," Shay said.

"And then what happens if Jason wants his room here?" Tina asked.

"I've got some ideas about it. Now, don't you girls worry," he reassured them. "Years ago, Jason mentioned

Layne to me often enough. He might not have said how he felt about her, but that was clear to me. Her feelings were even more obvious. Everything Shay just said only makes me more convinced, and talking to Jason this morning did, too. Despite their scrapping, I can see those two are meant for each other." He smiled. "I'll come up with some way to keep them together until they finally see it for themselves."

THE WEEKEND PASSED in a blur for Layne as she drifted in and out of a feverish sleep.

When she awoke again, muted sunlight was seeping into the living room around the edges of the drawn curtains. The only other light came from the glow of the television screen. Jason sat in the armchair with the remote in his hand, flipping through channels.

"You awake?" he said.

"Barely. The kids?" she asked, her voice still raspy.

"Asleep in their room."

She looked again at the sunlight edging the curtains. "What time is it?" she asked, her voice raspy. "What *day* is it?"

"Going on seven. And it's Monday."

She gasped and raised a hand to her head. "It can't be."

"Well, it is."

She recalled him bringing her mugs of soup to spoon up, cups of tea to drink, the baby to hold close for feedings. She had a dim memory of all that as well as a few trips down the hall to the bathroom. She also had the faint remembrance of hugging her son before Jason put him to bed each night.

Once or twice she had thought of calling her brother.

It surprised her that she hadn't heard from Cole or Tina, especially now the wedding was over. They all usually touched base with each other by phone every couple of days, or even in person when one or both of them stopped by SugarPie's.

But of course they had been busy at Garland Ranch all last week, between visiting with Tina's aunts and uncles, who had come to stay for the wedding, and preparing for the big day. And by now Cole had his hands full filling in for Pete while he was on his honeymoon.

They had probably taken yesterday as a well-deserved day of rest.

In any case, she couldn't have asked either of them for help.

As hard as it was to admit, under the circumstances, Jason had timed his reappearance in Cowboy Creek perfectly.

When she ran her hand over her face, Jason glanced her way.

"I was really out of it this past couple of days, wasn't I?"

He nodded. "That you were."

She groaned. "I've got to get myself together. Get back to work. I need to call Sugar."

"No, you don't. She called you. I told her you were still out of it."

"You talked to her without telling me she was on the phone?"

"I tried twice to wake you and then gave up. You wouldn't budge. Sugar said take all the time you need."

"I don't *have* time, Jason. The bills won't pay themselves."

"In your state, you'll be lucky to get dressed on your own."

"Well, don't worry," she said, keeping her voice light, "I won't be asking for your help." She retied the robe she had kept on during the worst of her chills. "I could use a change of clothes, though, that's for sure." A dim memory edged into her mind, and she looked over at him again. "Those cowboy pajamas you picked out for Scott to wear last night... They're his favorites."

"He told me."

What else had her chatty son said? "You took care of both the kids all this time."

"Yeah."

She ought to be upset by the high-handed way he had walked in and taken charge of her life. But at the moment, she couldn't manage to gather enough strength for that. She shifted on the couch, trying to sit upright. He leaned across the coffee table and adjusted the pillow behind her. "Thanks."

He nodded silently and gestured toward a mug near her on the table.

Apple juice, still cold from the refrigerator. Greedily, she drank some down and let it soothe her aching throat. She tensed, waiting for the juice to hit her stomach, anticipating the urge to bolt. Nothing happened—thank goodness.

"In case you're wondering, your trips down the hall these past couple of days have been flu-symptom free," Jason said.

"What?"

"You've provided status updates."

She groaned. Forget whatever Scott might have said

to him in conversation. What else had *she* revealed? "That comes from being a mom," she muttered.

"Yeah, and from changing too danged many dirty diapers, I'd bet."

"You're racking up experience in that, too."

"Well, I'm not a greenhorn anymore, that's for sure." He looked back at the television, but not quickly enough to hide the hint of a smile.

She frowned. He was certainly happy this morning, probably because he saw the end of his babysitting services in sight.

The thought triggered another memory of the past few days. She had managed to stay awake during Shay's visit, but once she and Jason were alone with the kids, grogginess had overtaken her. She had given in to it... as if it felt safe for her to sleep with him here, natural for him to watch the kids.

Those thoughts went beyond crazy. And were much too dangerous.

Jason sat with his gaze glued to the television again, his thumb busy on the remote. "It always made me nuts when you'd do that," she said.

"Do what?"

"Pause to watch a few minutes of a show, then flip to the next channel just when it was getting interesting."

He shrugged. "What's wrong with that?"

"You never settled long enough to find out what happened." Just as he hadn't stayed long enough with her to see if their marriage would work. But how could she blame him for that? Her throat tightened. She took a sip of juice.

He didn't say another word.

She frowned. Somehow, even in her clouded state

these past two days, she had noted something different about him. After Shay's departure, she recalled their heated argument and his flat refusal to leave her alone with the kids. He had gone to her room to get a fresh cloth for the baby. And he had come back quieter. More thoughtful. More subdued.

At that point, he couldn't have known his babysitting job would drag on for another two days. Maybe he had already regretted insisting he would stay. How must he feel now?

"All that sleep did me a lot of good. You could—"

"Don't even suggest it."

He settled back in the chair as if to keep her from forcibly throwing him out. The thought made her wince. "I'm sorry about...our conversation the other day."

"Conversation?"

"What I said to you."

"Such as?"

She stiffened. "You're going to make me spell it out?"

"Why not? You didn't have any problem saying it the first time."

"All right, I called you a sperm donor. Maybe I shouldn't have said it. And I've just apologized. But it doesn't matter now. You were right—our relationship's old history. And that makes me question again why you're here."

He froze for a long moment. The television stayed on the same channel, tuned to an early weather report. The blonde with the toothpaste-ad smile assured viewers temperatures would be mild for the next few days—no surprise for New Mexico even in the middle of winter.

The silence stretched on. Whatever he was going to say, she wouldn't like hearing it. She wondered how the temperature would be between them once he finally gave her an answer. Already, she could feel herself growing warm. Uncomfortable. Agitated.

Chapter Six

Despite the years they'd been apart, he was discovering he still knew Layne. Which meant he knew his announcement wouldn't sit well with her at all. Unlike a few days ago when she'd asked him straight-out why he'd come back, she didn't look on the verge of fainting. And there were no kids in the room to interrupt and save him from having to answer. He had no way of getting out of this conversation.

That didn't mean he had to unload everything at once.

"I want to make up for lost time," he said simply.

"What?"

He almost laughed as he took in the same look of dismay he had seen when he'd mentioned her bathroom reports. Did she think "lost time" meant getting together with her again? The laughter curdled in the back of his throat. He swallowed hard. "I want to pay off the child support I already owe you and make arrangements to keep paying going forward."

"I don't want money from you, Jason. I've never wanted it. You knew that."

"How could I not know," he said bitterly, "when one after another, all my letters kept coming back. Guess I should have expected that. You'd made it plain enough after you turned down my offer of alimony and child support—when you swore to me you'd be better off as a single parent. None of those are things I'm likely ever to forget." To this day, he could also remember the reactions that had surged inside him. Anger. Disgust. Disillusionment.

Coming back here couldn't change any of that, couldn't erase it as if it had never been. All he could do now was put the memories aside and go forward. "That's all old history, too. I was young and dumb enough— and all right, angry enough at the time—to take you at your word about not needing the support. Now I'm not."

"Thanks anyway."

His fingers tightened around the remote. The television volume jumped a few notches. The sound of a police siren whined through the room. He lowered the volume again and tossed the remote onto the coffee table. "If you can take money from Jill's daddy—"

"Who said I'm accepting anything from him?"

Damn. She supported not one but two kids on her own? "What happened between you?" He hadn't meant to ask, but now the question hung there, he realized how much he wanted to know.

"That's not any of your business. And I told you, he's out of the picture."

"All the more reason for me to man up and take responsibility."

"I don't need your money. I do fine."

"Mommy."

Scott's voice startled them both. They turned toward the door to the hall. The boy stood framed in the doorway, rubbing his eyes just the way he'd done the past couple of nights after Jason settled him in bed.

Tucking his son in at night and reading him a bed-time story—two things he'd never thought he would get the chance to do.

Two things he'd probably never do again if Layne insisted on going back to work and kicking him out of her life.

"The sheriff is coming?" Scott asked.

"No, honey," Layne said. "That siren you heard was on television."

"Oh." He crossed the room and climbed up onto the edge of the couch. Layne still sat back with the pillow against the arm of the chair. Scott leaned against her side.

Jason eyed the boy, then looked at Layne again and said quietly, "I'm not buying into your doing fine, either. Not when you wake up in a sickbed and the first thoughts you have—after your kids—are about the bills you need to pay."

"Everybody's got bills."

"Right. Responsibilities they take care of. So let me take care of mine." He needed her agreement on this. His self-respect demanded it.

But what exactly had he expected? That he could waltz into town and explain all this to Layne and receive her smile and a handshake? Gentlemen settled their arguments that way. But Layne sure was no gentleman. And she sure didn't seem interested in ending this argument.

Even fighting the flu—and *still* fighting him—she was a beautiful woman. She'd always been beautiful to him.

The thoughts had him shifting his gaze back to the television. Physical responses had him shifting in his seat. Neither reaction was going to get him anywhere. He knew better than most what happened when Layne's stubborn streak or his own took control of their relationship. Plenty of times, they'd dug in their heels over something, fought it out, then made up and made love.

He didn't have those options anymore. He had to think with his head, not with his…gut reactions. Had to rely on what he knew about her.

"Look, you told me you waitress for Sugar, which means you don't bring in a salary. You work for an hourly wage and tips, right?"

She nodded.

"Then all these days away from the job had to have set you back. Let me tide you over until you get on your feet." *Let me get you used to accepting financial help from me. Because it's the least you deserve.* "If nothing else, I can buy a few groceries."

"I've got a full refrigerator and pantry."

"You think so?" He forced a smile. "Not since Scott and I have taken over the kitchen. We're a couple of growing boys. Right, pardner?" he asked, holding his hand palm-out toward Scott.

"Right!" the kid exclaimed, reaching up for a high five.

The sound of his laugh turned Jason's smile into a genuine grin.

"I forgot paper towels," Layne murmured.

They stood in the cereal aisle at the Local-General Store, Cowboy Creek's primary grocery store, known to the locals as the L-G.

"I'll backtrack and pick 'em up," Jason volunteered.

"Me, too, me, too," Scott insisted.

The idea of the pair of them wandering away together made her edgy, though she wasn't sure why. They had spent plenty of time together this week.

As they went past her and down the aisle behind her again, she caught sight of Shay approaching, carrying one of the L-G's small baskets. With a sigh of relief, she grabbed at what she hoped would be a good chance to chat. To get a break from thoughts of Jason.

Maybe not so much, judging by the first words out of Shay's mouth.

"Looks like you and Jason are a matched set again."

Avoiding Shay's eyes, Layne tightened her fingers on the shopping cart. "This is not what it looks like." Aware Jason and Scott might not have left the aisle or another customer might come up from behind her, she kept her voice low. "He just offered to drive me to the store." *And to pay for my groceries.*

The thought of that only increased her uneasiness. She couldn't let him walk in and take over her life. Especially not when she knew he would soon walk back out again.

"Jason's only helping me because I have to pick up such a large order," she said firmly. Why did she have the feeling she was trying to convince herself as much as Shay? "After all the soup I ate while I was sick, I need to make another big batch for the freezer." And to buy enough food to refill all the refrigerator and pantry shelves he and Scott had cleared. He hadn't been kidding about them decimating her groceries. After one glance, she had suddenly felt like Mother Hubbard with her bare cupboards.

He hadn't been wrong about her weakness from the flu, either. Though she had wanted to get moving again, it had taken her half the morning to feel strong enough to get dressed and attempt the trip to the store.

"He'll be leaving soon anyway, so there's no point in even talking about him. Thank you for stopping by with the cake," she added, moving the conversation in a safer direction, though even that made her uncomfortable. She had slept through both Shay's visit and Sugar's phone call yesterday. "I'm sorry I missed you. How was the wedding?"

At the Hitching Post's first official wedding reception the month before, Shay had helped serve. But at the Garland family wedding on Saturday, she had attended as a guest. Layne would have, too, if not for her bout with the flu.

"Jane looked elegant, of course," Shay said. "We knew she would. And Pete was his usual hunky self." As she rattled off details about the ceremony and reception, Layne smiled and nodded and attempted to keep her thoughts from straying to the paper products aisle. "And through it all," Shay continued, "you'd have thought Jed was the hero of the hour."

"Did somebody say 'hero'?"

Layne jumped. She hadn't heard either Jason or Scott come up behind her. "Shay's talking about Jed Garland."

"He's so happy about all his granddaughters getting engaged," Shay said.

"I hear he had a hand in that," Jason said. "Or so he tells me."

"Well, if he didn't," Layne said, "there has to be some wedding magic in the air around the Hitching Post."

Abruptly, Shay hefted her small basket. "I'd better get home and drop these off with my grandmother before I head in to work. Grandma Mo wants to see you one day soon, Scott." She tousled Scott's hair, gave Layne a smile, and nodded farewell to Jason.

As Shay walked away, Layne thought about what she had said a few minutes ago.

Looks like you and Jason are a matched set again.

She hadn't liked hearing that. She hadn't liked knowing how much she wished it were true. How could she have gone from wanting nothing to do with him, to having thoughts like this?

Jill let out a squawk and began to wriggle in her carrier in the front seat of the grocery cart. Layne popped the pacifier into the baby's mouth. "I've got the cereal. We're done. But we'd better speed things up at the checkout if we want to make it home in time for me to feed the baby."

"Speed them up?" Jason exhaled heavily and plopped the paper towels into the cart. "I've been running up and down aisles after Scott. I don't know how you do it with two of them and only one of you."

"I manage. Normally, my shopping wouldn't take this long, but we had a lot of extra food to buy."

"Told you Scott and I cleaned out the cupboards." He frowned. "You look about ready to drop."

"I'm tired," she admitted. Even as she spoke, she felt more of her energy draining away.

"All right, then let's get you back home." He took the cart from her and went in the direction of the checkout counter.

While she was grateful not to have to push the heavy cart, she missed having it to hold on to. With the way she felt now, she needed it to prop herself up. Slowly, she followed Jason and the kids down the aisle.

No matter what she had said to Shay about Jason

leaving soon, this everyday trip to the store had left her daydreaming of what it would be like to have him stay. Of what their life might have been like if he had never left. Their few days together had offered her a taste, a tease, the tiniest bit of temptation. But along with the daydreams had come a fear big enough to eclipse all the pleasure she had felt.

She was getting too comfortable with Jason again. Becoming too involved. Being reminded much too poignantly of the boy she used to love.

The boy who had stopped loving her.

JASON GRIPPED THE steering wheel and listened to the wail of the baby in the backseat of his pickup truck. Somehow, in the small space the noise sounded magnified. As the noise increased, the truck windows seemed to shiver.

Across the cab, Layne's gaze met his.

Earlier, as they had left her apartment for the grocery store, she had pointed out the kids' car seats near the front door. She had strapped both Scott and Jill into those seats for the ride to the L-G. Now she had just finished settling the baby again for the ride home. Or tried to anyway.

Jill's screech rose a notch. He'd have sworn his eardrums rattled.

"She's hungry. I'll have to feed her here," Layne announced. She opened the passenger door and returned to the backseat.

Though he tried to ease his stranglehold on the steering wheel, he could think of nothing else to do with his hands. Or of anywhere else to direct his gaze. With the truck in Park in the middle of the L-G's lot, he couldn't pretend a need to keep his eyes on the road.

He shot a couple of quick glances into the rearview mirror to check on Scott. The boy sat running one of his toy cars along the restraining bar of his car seat.

"Could you get me a cloth from the diaper bag?" Layne asked.

He began to reach across the front seat for the bag, forgetting for a moment that he was strapped in place as securely as Scott was fastened into his car seat. He thumbed open the clasp of his seat belt and grabbed the bag. A second later, he reached back over the bench seat and held out the cloth to Layne.

"Thanks," she said. "Sorry about this."

Not as sorry as he was.

In the past few days, every time she'd fed the baby, he had found a reason to move away—checking something on the stove, helping Scott with his motorway, flipping through the television channels at lightning speed.

He wasn't a man given to analyzing his emotions, but it had been obvious those previous incidents involved physical responses to the thought of seeing Layne half-undressed. Now...

Now his reactions came from somewhere deeper, from something more, from knowing he couldn't look at the woman he'd once loved and watch her nurse a baby that wasn't his. And that was his own damned fault, because he *could* have watched her with his own child. But he had walked away from the chance. Had given up that right.

"I don't think we'll be long," Layne said. "My Jill's a quick eater when she's hungry. Aren't you, sweetie? And Jason..." A hint of amusement laced her tone. "You can turn around now."

"I'm adjusting the heater," he said, hoping she believed him. A second later, he turned halfway and settled back against the driver's door.

She had draped the cloth loosely over the baby, shielding her from the sun streaming in the truck's window and from the gaze of any shoppers in the L-G's parking lot.

"She's a good eater as well as a quick one, huh?" he asked.

"Yes. Almost as good as you and Scott."

He couldn't help but laugh. "Then you'll really be looking at some grocery bills soon, won't you?" When he saw the frown lines between her eyes, his smile slid away.

No, he wasn't a man to analyze emotions, yet he could tell in his gut something wasn't right. No matter how much she denied it, she was hurting for money, and being off from her job had only made things worse. Her situation—her current situation—had nothing to do with him. But who knew how things would have turned out if he'd stuck around.

He had plenty to answer for from the past. Maybe he'd been wrong to walk away years ago. To give up all those chances.

Now he just wanted the opportunity to make something right.

Chapter Seven

Layne glanced across the kids' room to the crib, where Jill slept peacefully in the same position she had curled into a half hour earlier.

She had already emptied the contents of the kids' hamper into the laundry basket now balanced against her hip. Not wanting to wake her daughter, she almost tiptoed from the room and down the hall.

When she reached the entrance to the living room, she paused. At the scene inside the room, her chest squeezed tight as if she had just sprinted down the hallway and couldn't catch her breath.

Her son knelt on the floor between the couch and the coffee table. One of his favorite storybooks lay open in front of him on the table. Jason sat on the couch behind Scott, leaning over his shoulder. As they focused on the pages, both their faces wore the identical expression of concentrated interest. She had seen that once before, noting that anyone looking at them would assume they were related, would probably realize they were father and son. But no one could guess the two of them had met only days ago.

Her eyes misted. She blinked the moisture away. She couldn't let these few days weaken her resolve.

Years ago, she had seen the end of her marriage to Jason coming. There was no way she could avoid or deny it. Worse, she had known their relationship was a mistake from the start.

Both her relationships had been mistakes.

She had married for all the wrong reasons, the first time because she was wildly in love with her high-school sweetheart but too young to understand *permanent* didn't mean *perfect*. The second time, she wanted to provide a father for the child Jason had walked away from. Not once but twice, she had put her faith in men who couldn't be trusted.

It wasn't enough that she had failed herself with her bad choices. She had failed her children, too. And if she had learned one thing from the experiences, it was never to let herself fall for a man again.

Especially a man who had already made one fall hurt so much.

Across the room, Jason pointed over Scott's shoulder to the book. "What's that?"

"A baby cow."

"And what does a baby cow say?"

"Moo-oo-oo." Scott laughed. "Moo-oo-oo. That's *em-mm-mm*."

"You're pretty smart, aren't you?"

Her son nodded. "Yep. Mommy says. And Mommy says a baby cow drinks milk. *Em-mm-mm.* Milk. Like Jill drinks milk."

Seeing Jason's now-frozen expression, Layne couldn't hold back a laugh that verged on a sob. She had caught that same uneasy look on his face when she'd had to feed Jill in the truck. She couldn't blame his awkwardness on the fact he hadn't been here after Scott's birth—not when she had seen and heard how uncomfortable other men often felt at being around a nursing mom in public. But all the same, she wished he had been there for her son.

At her laugh, Jason had looked up and glanced in her direction. Frowning, he rose from the couch and crossed the room. He reached out to take the laundry basket from her. "Where do you want this?"

She would have argued but suspected that wouldn't do her any good. And she didn't have the energy. She gestured toward the kitchen. "There's a washer and dryer in a closet in there. Scott, we'll be right back." She followed Jason into the kitchen and gestured to the closet door. "You can just set it down there, thanks."

"There's a washer *and* a dryer in that closet?" he asked, sounding as if he didn't believe her.

"Yes." She moved past him and opened the door to show him the stacked appliances. "No running to the coin laundry, the way we had to do when we were married."

"That's a real shame."

He went perfectly still as if he had blurted the words without thinking.

For that matter, so had she, not stopping to recall what happened all those times they had gone to the laundry together. Once she loaded the washing machine and fed it the required detergent and coins, she and Jason would move to the table used for folding clothes. He would lift her up to sit on the edge of the table, then move in close for a kiss.

At the thought, her legs suddenly trembled. She took her usual seat at the kitchen table and looked across at the chair he had been using since he'd come back home…back to town. The chair where he'd plopped his Stetson after he'd carried in the sacks of groceries for her.

He had done so much for her and the kids in these past few days. She couldn't—wouldn't—be in his debt. Somehow, she would need to find ways to pay him back. She looked past him toward the closet. "I'll be washing shirts and sweaters after lunch if you want to add anything to the load."

After a moment, he said, "No need to trouble yourself."

"It's no trouble. I'm running the washer anyway."

"I thought you'd gone to get some rest."

"I did rest. For a while. I'm getting as bad as Jill with her nap times. I need to stop resting so much and get back on my feet."

The way I'd done after you *left.*

She couldn't let herself forget that.

Abruptly, he crossed to the chair and picked up his Stetson. "You know, it's almost time for lunch. How about I grab something for us from SugarPie's?"

"But you just bought all those groceries. I didn't want you to pay for them to begin with." Even as she said the words, she almost cringed. Her voice sounded too high, her tone too sharp, laced with feelings she couldn't identify. She only hoped Jason hadn't heard the difference, too.

He grabbed the pen and notepad she kept on the counter near the phone. "Right now, I could do with one of Sugar's sub sandwiches. Let's go see what Scott wants."

Obviously, he was in a big hurry to leave. Before she could blink, he had gone through the doorway into the living room. As she stared after him, she struggled to make sense of her feelings.

Was she annoyed at him for wanting some distance? Or upset with herself for not wanting him to go?

THE FIRST PERSON Jason spotted at SugarPie's was none other than Jed Garland. There were only a few booths in the place, most of them still unoccupied. Jed sat sprawled comfortably in the last one in the row as if he were a king surveying his kingdom—as the folks in town had always thought of him. Anybody with a problem or a question, anyone looking for a favor or a good turn, knew they would get what they needed from Jed.

The hefty gray-haired woman nearly filling the seat across from him owned both the sandwich shop and the bakery that shared the same building. She wasn't queen of Cowboy Creek, but in her own way, Sugar Conway could hold court, too.

Jed gave him a regal wave. Sugar glanced over her shoulder.

He headed their way.

As he approached the booth, Sugar looked him up and down. "Well, here's the man of the hour," she proclaimed with her Southern twang, making him wonder just what Jed had said to her about him. "I've kept your seat warm for you." She eased sideways from behind the tabletop and waved him toward the bench.

"I'm not staying long." He took the vacant seat. "Just going to order some sandwiches to take home…that is, take back to Layne's."

"And how is she doing?"

"Much better." He paused. This was Layne's employer. "She's still not too steady on her feet, though. I can't see her carrying trays for a while."

"Oh, you can't, huh?" Sugar rested her hands on the edge of the table. He swore he heard wood groan from the weight. "I don't know what you can see or what you plan to do." She had leaned closer and lowered her already soft voice. Her drawl sounded more pronounced. "But I'll tell you this. Layne's a good girl, and she's been through a hard time these past few years. A *very* hard time, mostly thanks to you."

He met her gaze as steadily as he could. "You're blaming everything that's happened to her on me." But why wouldn't she? Hadn't he come close to doing that himself?

"I blame you for leaving her and your baby." She shook her head sadly. "After that day you two were in here, so happy about having Scott on the way, I can't believe you walked out on her."

"I didn't…" But he did.

Across the table, Jed held up a palm. "Maybe Jason ought to place his order before you get too busy with the lunchtime crowd."

"Good idea." Jason had slid the note Layne had given him into his shirt pocket. He fished it out now, recited what she had written for herself and Scott, and added his own sandwich to the order.

Without bothering to take the note or to write anything on her order pad, Sugar nodded and stomped away.

He exhaled in a huff. "I don't know what she meant about keeping my seat warm," he said, trying to laugh off his own uneasiness. "To me, it sounded more like putting me in the hot seat."

"You ought to be used to that, considering you got yourself into it often enough with Layne."

"Yeah." He forced a laugh. "Between that and the doghouse, never a dull moment."

Never a lack of clean clothes, either, thanks to those frequent trips to the laundry. All these years later, even her mention of the place had him breathing hard. He rubbed his forehead, as if he could erase the memories.

"She *is* feeling better," he assured Jed. She would have to be, if she was up to doing laundry, wouldn't she?

"That's good."

"Yeah. I'll be out of her hair soon and over at the Hitching Post. Once she's past the point of needing a caretaker." No matter what she said about getting back on her feet, he wasn't leaving until he was sure she wouldn't have a relapse.

Unfortunately, he'd gone well past the point of needing to back off himself. They had too many memories between them, had set themselves up for too many situations they needed to tiptoe around. One false step, and all his plans would blow up in his face. And the longer he stayed near her, the greater his chances of that.

"I don't think it's so much a caretaker she needs," Jed said. "But a young mother like Layne, on her own with two kids, it's a hard life. She does need someone to give her a hand."

"Yeah." He fiddled with the napkin holder set to one side of the table. "What's up with her baby's father? Who was it she married?" *If* she had married the man. He realized he didn't know even that for sure.

"Terry Johansen."

He remembered Johansen from high school, a tall thin

guy interested only in computer games and the school chess club. Layne could have done better.

Then again, she'd most likely thought she had already done worse. With him.

"It wasn't a good match," Jed continued, "not even from the start. You know Layne, loyal to a fault. She seemed determined to make things work, but they split up before the girl was born. Terry took care of the doctor bills, and then he took off."

Another deadbeat dad. No need to hear the man say the words aloud.

"Layne mentioned he doesn't help her out." Dammit, he was fishing for info, wanting to find out what Jed knew. Wanting to know just what she might have said about *him*, too.

"Never heard a word of that. Layne will talk about her kids, but she's not one to wear her heart on her sleeve about the past. Except for maybe with Cole, she usually keeps those things to herself." Jed set aside the coffee mug he'd been holding and folded his arms on the tabletop.

Here came the heavy hand holding the whip. The reading of the riot act. The former boss's version of Sugar's so-called seat-warming.

"You know," Jed started off mildly, "you ought to consider giving your relationship with Layne another try."

His jaw nearly dropped. "That wouldn't work in a million years."

"I don't see why not, if you put some thought behind it."

Even as he shook his head, he couldn't keep from

wondering what it would be like to be on good terms with Layne again. For more than just their son's sake.

Sugar returned to the table with his order, saving him from having to respond to Jed. Saving him from his own dangerous thoughts. He would be a fool to make the same mistake twice by getting involved with his ex-wife.

"I'd better be moving along." In more ways than one. He took the sack from Sugar and rose from his seat. "Scott's hungry, and Layne might need another nap."

"Didn't you say she was doing much better?" Sugar asked.

"I did. I also said she wasn't too steady on her feet." Neither was he, at the moment.

"Then you'd best hightail it back there," Jed advised.

"And not go rushing off again, if she still needs help." Her parting shot delivered, Sugar turned away.

He followed her to the counter to pay for his order. As he waited for change, he thought about Jed's suggestion.

He had already acknowledged Layne was more beautiful than ever. He just hadn't allowed himself to admit he was as hot for her now as he was in their high-school and newlywed days.

What kind of man was he to be having thoughts like that about an overtired, overworked and ill single mom? About a woman who wouldn't have allowed him a cup of coffee if not for the fact he had taken over her kitchen? Not that either of them had had a choice about that.

"Here you go." Sugar handed him his change. "And you tell Layne not to hurry back until she's ready, y'hear?"

"I'll do that." He pocketed the coins. As he slid the bills into his worn wallet, he thought about the birth announcement tucked inside.

No matter what Jed thought or where his own thoughts had taken him, he couldn't have a relationship with Layne. He couldn't take that risk.

He wouldn't let anything jeopardize this second chance with his son.

JASON RETURNED TO Layne's apartment and handed out the sandwiches.

While Layne quietly gathered plates and utensils and poured their drinks, Scott chattered away. He held the floor through most of the meal. With his sister still asleep in their room, he might be taking advantage of having his mama's attention to himself. Jason could understand that. He felt a surge of…something every time Layne looked his way.

"I go to school today, Mommy?" Scott asked.

"Yeah," Jason said. He stowed the plastic-wrapped half of Scott's sandwich in the restocked refrigerator. "Didn't you tell me he goes to preschool? Are they still off for the holidays?"

She shook her head. "We call it school because he has lessons."

"Like the big kids," Scott put in.

"Exactly." She smiled at him, then glanced over at Jason. "He and Jill go to day care in a private home that doesn't run on holidays. The woman who owns it also watches them for me when I work a night shift."

"Miss Rhea," Scott said.

"That's right." She gave him another smile before she continued, "I kept Scott home when I got sick. The first day, it hit me so hard, I wasn't up to getting him ready to go out. And then I wanted to make sure he hadn't caught the bug, too." She turned back to Scott.

"No Miss Rhea's today. You stay home one more day and you can go tomorrow."

"Does the kid understand what *tomorrow* means?"

Layne gave him a level look. "Ask him."

"What's *tomorrow*, Scott?" He was startled to see the boy's frown. It matched the expression he'd occasionally caught in his own mirror. Now, he had an answer to his best friend's question about which of his parents Scott took after.

"I go to sleep," the boy said, "and then I open my eyes and see the sun again." He had almost chanted the reply. Layne must have taught him that, too.

She rose from her seat and carried a couple of plates to the sink.

He grabbed their drinking glasses.

They cleaned off the table and counters as if they had worked together every day for years. In the close quarters of her small kitchen, it wouldn't have taken but a half step at any given moment for him to brush up against her. To set her up on the counter the way he'd always hoisted her onto the table at the laundry. And to settle his hips between her knees as he leaned in to take a kiss.

And every time those thoughts crossed his mind, he had to remind himself to keep his hands to himself.

Alone, she would have been fair game. With a couple of kids, she was off-limits. Even if she hadn't been out of his reach, he had to focus on his son.

These few days together had already convinced him he needed more than a weeklong visit each summer. He wanted an ongoing connection to his child and hoped he and Layne could at least agree to that. Making a move on her wouldn't help his cause in the slightest.

While she finished loading the dishwasher, he leaned

back against the counter. "Maybe you ought to take a nap, too, while Jill's asleep," he suggested. "I'll keep Scott occupied."

She turned to him, her expression blank. "I thought you were leaving after lunch. You said you planned to drive out to Jed's."

"I did say that. But I thought I'd stick around for a while yet. You've been up and moving around since we left for the store this morning. I figure you're due for some downtime."

She shook her head. "I'm fine."

"Then, since you're not sending Scott back to school until tomorrow, why don't I take him to the park for a while?"

"No."

"Yay!"

The contradictory responses came as if in the same breath. Before Jason could address either one, Layne turned to Scott. "Honey, you go play with your cars in the living room, okay?"

"I go to park with Jason."

"Not today."

"I go tomorrow?"

Smart kid.

"You have school again tomorrow, remember?" she said. "You go ahead to the living room. Mommy will be there in just a minute."

He shot a look toward Jason but said nothing else. He slid from his seat and left the kitchen.

Very smart kid.

Layne turned to him. "When you have children, you learn to be careful what you say in front of them."

Damn. Mama wasn't bad herself. In one sentence,

she'd managed both to slap him with a warning and to ignore the fact Scott was his son.

He swallowed his anger and said mildly, "I already have a kid, and I'm trying to get to know him. What's the harm in taking a walk in the park?"

"The harm is that raising kids isn't just about a walk in the park. But you wouldn't know that." She took a deep breath and let it out again. "Jason, don't do this. You've had some time with Scott. And that's as far as this will go. Because *you're* going to go."

"Not before we see the sun a few times again."

"Don't try to be funny. There's nothing amusing about this conversation." This time, her breath sounded shaky. "Please. Don't make this harder than it has to be. I'm going to go out into the living room with Scott. Come with me and say goodbye. You're not staying, in my house or in Cowboy Creek. And I won't let Scott get close to another man only to see him walk out of his life."

"I'm not just 'another man.'"

"You are, to my son. As far as he knows, he has one parent—me. And I'm the only one he's going to know."

Chapter Eight

Jason stared into the mirror behind the bar without seeing much of anything. He'd come to the Cantina, Cowboy Creek's only restaurant-slash-saloon for a place to hang out for a while. To get some distance from Layne. And to give her a chance to settle down.

No matter what she said, he wasn't leaving her alone with the kids for the night. If his own conscience hadn't already ensured that—and it had—his conversations with Jed and Sugar would have closed the deal.

From behind him, someone clapped a heavy hand on his shoulder, startling him into knocking over his bottle of pop. As he made a grab for the bottle, a man slid onto the empty bar stool beside his. In the mirror opposite, he caught the glint of a badge on a uniform shirt.

Jeez, had Layne called in the law?

He'd left her apartment peacefully enough, considering she'd kicked him out yet again.

With Jed most likely still holding court at SugarPie's and Jed's ranch manager, Pete, off on his honeymoon, there had been no point heading to the Hitching Post. And he couldn't think of anywhere else to go to kill some time. The Cantina had the added benefit of keeping him from running into anyone he knew. It was long enough after noon that the lunchtime crowd had cleared out, yet too early for the dinners and drinking to begin.

But in a small town like this one, he should have known better than to expect he could escape notice. Especially from the law.

He eyed the man on the bar stool, who now sat chugalugging from a bottle of water. Then he set the bottle on the bar and held out his hand to Jason. "Long time no see."

As recognition hit, he blinked. He shook hands with the deputy. "Mitch Weston, a sheriff? I can't believe my eyes."

"Believe it. And I'm new to the department but not to the work. Before this, I was with the LAPD." The bartender approached, and Mitch turned to deliver his lunch order.

Jason's path had crossed with Mitch's often enough all through school, and once he'd started wrangling at Garland Ranch, they had run across each other frequently there. Mitch had been good with livestock but always more interested in horsepower than horses. When he turned back again, Jason said, "Don't tell me Cowboy Creek's got a motorcycle unit."

"We're not big enough for that. Besides, my biking days are over. We run to patrol cars, and that's about it." He reached for his water bottle. "What brings you back to town? Or do I need to ask?"

The other man had been around in the days when he and Layne had started dating. Not answering, he took another swig of his pop.

"Jed says you'll be staying with us at the Hitching Post," Mitch added.

"'Us'?"

"Yeah. I'm marrying the last of his granddaughters. Technically, I'm bunking in with my folks until the wedding, but I spend more time out at the hotel than I do at home." Mitch grinned. "In case you hadn't heard yet, Jed has turned into the town matchmaker. He's run out of eligible family members, but that won't stop him. If you're not interested, I'd advise you to watch your step or, before you know it, he'll have you matched up with the nearest unattached female."

What would he think if he knew Jed was already in there swinging? "What else did he have to say?"

"Not much, except that you took a room at the Hitching Post, though nobody's seen anything of you out there yet. Cole thought you might be lying low because of him."

"Why would he think that?"

"He just found out you were back in town, and he's protective of his sister. You can't fault the man for that."

"Meaning, you can fault the other guy?"

Mitch shrugged. "I'm not making judgments. I wasn't around at all when Layne was married to you. Or to Terry, for that matter."

The bartender set a sack lunch on the counter in front of Mitch. He paid, grabbed the sack and stood. After the bartender went to take care of another customer a few stools away, Mitch turned back. "I'm staying neutral in this. And as Jed would put it, Cole's not gunning for bear, either. But I think he'll have a lot to say when you two meet. Luckily, he's too busy now with Pete on his honeymoon to get away from the ranch."

"Thanks for the warning."

"Just trying to keep the peace." Mitch grinned, then walked away.

What a helluva reception he'd gotten in Cowboy Creek today. Warnings from the local law. A caution from the sandwich shop owner. Advice from a man who couldn't possibly consider him a candidate for matchmaking services. And on top of all that, grief from the ex-wife who could keep him from his son.

Except for the last on that list, the rest of the folks in town had a point. Way back when, they'd known better than he had that his marriage wouldn't last. Now they knew how little chance he had of making up for walking away.

He turned back to his bottle of pop and thought about the day he'd spent at Greg's house swigging down a couple of beers. The picture he'd had in his head then of coming back to town sure wasn't matching reality— and he had no one to blame but himself.

To his discredit, he had thought only about himself and his son, about checking on his child's welfare, as if Layne played no part in his equation. Of course, to hear her tell it, *he* played no part in *hers*.

He had left her apartment this afternoon feeling the way he had when he'd walked away years ago. Except for the guilt. Back then, knowing their split was bitter but mutual, he'd felt justified. With the distance of a few years behind him, he realized he could have tried harder to fix things with her. To repair his marriage. He knew he needed to try harder to get along with her now.

He rubbed his jaw, took another drink and stared at himself in the mirror. Though he didn't look much different than he had before he'd left Cowboy Creek, he *was* different. He was a better man than the one who had left. And he needed to prove that to Layne.

FINISHED TYING JILL'S hat beneath her chin, Layne glanced across the living room. Scott leaned against the arm of the couch, head tilted down as he concentrated on buttoning his jacket. She smiled. Shoelaces were still beyond him, but he was proud of his ability to do up his buttons.

She looked at his expression, so like Jason's, and swallowed a sigh.

She regretted her knee-jerk response to Jason's request to take Scott to the park. He'd done so much for them, for her, these past few days. She had already acknowledged that to herself. But she couldn't forget their history. Couldn't let a few days of his attention wipe their slate clean.

A knock on the door startled her. Crazy as it seemed, that special, silly little tap had the power to make her heart pound. And foolish as it might be, she wished she could just stand there quietly and ignore the summons.

But of course, Scott ran to the door. "Who is that?" he called.

"It's...Jason."

Scott turned to her, and the look of excitement on his face made her heart thud. "Just a minute," she called. She lifted Jill in her carrier and crossed the room.

When she opened the door, Jason's eyebrows rose in surprise. He gestured to her and Scott dressed in jackets, and to Jill tucked cozily in her carrier beneath a baby blanket. "Going somewhere?"

She flushed, her cheeks growing so warm, she thought she might be having a relapse. The truth was, she needed to get out of the house, to distract herself from thoughts of him. She had considered going to the park with the kids, but after the way she had refused to let him take Scott there, she couldn't do that. "We're taking a walk to SugarPie's."

"Are you up for it?"

"I'll have to be. I'm going a little stir-crazy here." She hesitated. "What brought you back again?"

He hefted the duffel bag she hadn't noticed he was carrying. "I changed my mind. If the offer's still open, I'll take you up on washing some of my T-shirts." Before she could answer, he had stepped inside and set the bag on the floor beside the couch.

She had already finished the load of shirts, but she had plenty of other laundry to do. And she *had* also acknowledged that she needed to pay him back for his help. "Yes, the offer's open. But the kids are ready to go. If you can handle the washer on your own, feel free—"

"No problem. We can run the load when we get back." He plucked the handle of the carrier from her arm.

"You don't need to go—"

"Jason come, too?" Scott asked.

"Yes," he said firmly, "Jason come, too. We didn't have dessert after lunch, did we?"

Scott laughed, shaking his head. "*De-e-e.* Didn't have dessert."

"I think we need some, don't you?"

"Yes!"

Swallowing a protest, she followed them both from the apartment. She owed Jason for the groceries, and he had insisted on paying for lunch, too. The least she could do was take care of dessert.

She gestured to the carriage sitting just outside the door. "I was going to put Jill in this."

"Got it."

By the time she locked the door, Jason had tucked

Jill into the carriage and he and Scott had started off in the direction of Canyon Road, Cowboy Creek's main street. Scott walked beside Jason with one hand on the handle of the carriage.

With Jason shortening his steps to match her son's, she easily caught up to them.

They walked along together as if they were simply out for their usual stroll. Half of her wanted to believe in the fantasy. The other half of her wanted to call off this trip—this farce—and go home.

The afternoon sun was strong enough to combat the January chill in the air. It just couldn't do much about the shiver running through her. She crossed her arms over her chest and kept moving.

"You cold?" Jason asked. He wore no jacket, just the T-shirt he'd put on that morning.

"I'm fine," she said. It was partly true. Whether her reaction had come from pleasure or apprehension, she certainly wouldn't admit either possibility to Jason.

What she *should* do was tell him to turn the carriage over to her and then go on his way. She didn't want him getting more involved with her children. Considering their history, anyone would understand her feelings. And yet there were things she *did* want that didn't make any sense.

"I'd forgotten how quiet it is in Cowboy Creek," he said.

Not a car came down the side street, not a pedestrian walked in sight. Not even a dog barked anywhere within hearing.

"That's why I like this neighborhood. It's quiet. Safe for the kids."

"You've lived here for a while."

He made it a statement, not a question, but she knew what he was asking. And what was the point of hiding the truth? "Just since my second divorce." She looked sideways at him. "Where's home for you nowadays?"

"I don't have a home." She caught the bitterness in his tone. Then he laughed, and she realized she must have been mistaken. "Unless you call a bunkhouse full of cowboys a home."

"I suppose it is, if that's where you sleep every night."

He glanced at her as if he suspected a double meaning from the comment. When she said nothing else, he shrugged. "To tell the truth, over the past few years, I've probably slept in my truck more than I have in the bunkhouse."

Scott gasped. "Go to sleep in a *truck*?"

"I sure do," he confirmed.

"Mommy, I can have a truck, too?"

"I don't think so, honey. It wouldn't fit in your bedroom. And where would we put Jill's crib?"

"In my *truck*."

She and Jason both laughed.

She blinked and looked away. Scott's questions had reminded her of the caution she'd given Jason about watching what he said in front of kids. She had been unforgivably offensive to him—again. Somehow, she couldn't seem to stop crossing the line between asserting her rights and fighting a long-dead battle.

A slight breeze ruffled the loose edge of Jill's blanket. She reached over to tuck the cover into the carriage just as Jason reached down. Their hands collided, his fingers warm against hers. She shoved her hand into her jacket pocket. He tucked the blanket in and checked that the baby was covered, too, as if he'd done it a hundred times before.

At the crosswalk, Scott reached up to take Jason's hand, the way he had been taught to do with her whenever they crossed a street.

She wanted to pull her son's hand away from Jason's just as she had done with her own. But how could she protest without confusing Scott?

She was already confused enough herself. Almost, she wished Jason had never come back. Almost, she wished he had already gone home. He *would* go. That was inevitable. He had always been there for the fun times and in the short term. But when things got tough, he bolted.

Taking care of the kids while she was sick couldn't be classified as a pleasure in anyone's book, yet he'd done what he could for them. A walk to the sandwich shop wasn't much of a hot time, either. Yet, here he was.

And almost, she wished she could trust him to be around to share *all* the simple, everyday events in her life.

THEY HADN'T MADE it as far as SugarPie's, after all. When they had turned the corner onto Canyon Road, Scott had spotted the Big Dipper. He set his sights on going there, and his mama had gone along with the change in plans.

Jason didn't mind, either. A banana split wouldn't have been his first choice of dessert in January, but it never dropped off his personal menu. He wondered how much of Layne's agreement was driven by the boy's eagerness to have ice cream and how much of it came from her need to sit down.

They were the only ones in the place, which allowed

her to argue with him about who would pay for their order.

"You bought my groceries," she said in a low voice when Shay had moved away to assemble his banana split. "Getting dessert is the least I can do."

"You never pay when I'm with you at the Big Dipper," he said flatly.

Her face froze. She blinked once, then walked away to plop herself down at a nearby table.

They had left the carriage parked outside the shop. She set the baby carrier on the far edge of the table near the wall and took off the blanket. Scott settled down in a chair beside them with his ice cream cone.

The minute Jason joined them, Layne leaned forward and said quietly, "That wasn't necessary."

"Really? With the way Shay stood behind the counter giving me the evil eye?"

She shot a quick look toward the cash register, but he knew the other woman had disappeared through the doorway behind it into the back room.

"She didn't give you the evil eye."

"Close enough to it, and I wasn't about to stand down." He dug into his banana split and held up a mouthful of vanilla ice cream. "You sure you don't want any? I can always get another spoon."

"No, thanks."

"Too tame for you, huh? You always went for the fancy ones, the chocolate-marshmallow swirl or the pistachio-walnut-mint."

"I'm surprised you remembered." She didn't meet his eyes.

"Are you kidding? Those were premium flavors. I had to pay extra for 'em."

That got her looking at him. "Don't even try to make me feel guilty about that. Your banana splits and triple-dip sundaes cost three times as much as my cones."

He laughed and spooned up a mound of chocolate ice cream covered with whipped cream. "We spent plenty of time here in our dating days, didn't we?"

"It was everybody's favorite hangout."

"I'll agree with that. And I won't point out how you sidestepped the question."

When she turned her attention to the baby, he studied her. Layne's cheeks looked nearly as red as the cherry on his banana split. The color might have come from the cold outside or from flu symptoms she was hiding. He didn't know. But when she shivered again, he knew he couldn't attribute it to ice cream. She hadn't had any. "Are you sure you're not cold?"

She shook her head. "And I didn't sidestep your question. I'm just following a logical train of thought. We would probably have hung out at SugarPie's more often if she hadn't been so strict about all of us watching our manners."

"She sure hasn't let up any in that regard. When I went to get lunch, she gave me a piece of her mind. In that sweet Southern way of hers, of course."

"Really? About what?"

"About us. Or to be more accurate, about me." She didn't respond, but all that bright color drained from her cheeks. "About the way I'd left you. She doesn't think too kindly of me for that. And I just ran into Mitch Weston at the Cantina, and he tells me your brother doesn't have me too high on his list of favorites, either."

"Did you expect either of them would?"

Not wanting—or not able—to admit the truth to her, he stabbed at his ice cream with his spoon.

"Mommy." Scott held up his cone.

She took it from him and turned the cone slowly, making one long swipe with her tongue to clean up the dribbles of melting chocolate. Now *he* was the one shivering, but not from the temperature or the flu or his banana split.

"Yucky, Mommy." Scott smacked his sticky hands together.

Jason handed him a paper napkin from the dispenser at his elbow. The boy rubbed the napkin on his hands, then tossed it on the table—or tried to. The shredded paper clung to his ice-cream-covered fingers.

"I go wash."

Jason eyed the set of double doors at one end of the shop. They led to a hallway at the back of the building shared by the adjacent convenience store. At the midpoint of the hall the restrooms flanked the emergency exit. In their school days, kids looking for excitement sometimes ducked out through that exit with items they hadn't paid for. Or they visited the restrooms to carry out some minor act of vandalism. "I'll take Scott back to wash his hands." He was halfway out of his seat when Layne shook her head.

"I'll go with him."

Slowly, he sank back into his chair. "Okay. I'll watch Jill."

"I'll take her with us. She probably needs a change."

Scott had wandered off toward the direction of the hallway. He stood near the front counter, his sticky fingers splayed against the glass front. Shay wouldn't be too happy to see the results.

Jason looked at the baby, who was sleeping soundly, one fist curled under her chin. "She's out. No sense waking her up."

"She's used to it."

Layne reached for the handle of the carrier. He put his hand on her arm. "Wait a minute. What's going on?"

"Nothing." But again, she wouldn't look his way.

He stared at her. "*Something's* up. What, do you think I'll walk off with the baby? Or take Scott out the back entrance on our way to the bathrooms?"

"Don't be so silly," she snapped.

"Then don't be so damned stubborn," he shot back. "These past few days at your apartment, you were willing enough to take my help. But now we're out in public, something's different?"

"That has nothing to do with it."

"Then, what has?"

"This." She gestured with her free hand and shook her head in annoyance, but kept her voice down, probably thinking of Shay in the back room. "I've already thanked you for your help, but you know I wouldn't have accepted it if I could have found someone else. And I can't take this…this assumption you can just step into my life—our lives—and act like you've always been here. Like you never left."

"I'm not assuming anything, just going day by day. And being there for you, the way I have been for nearly a week now. I haven't done anything to make you think you can't trust me."

"But how do I know I can? You can't buy a person's trust with some groceries and an ice-cream cone. At least, not mine. You have to earn it."

He'd have called her on the statement, kept her from

walking away, insisted they finish the argument, except for the look on her face. For once, she hadn't managed to hide her emotions behind a blank expression. She hadn't turned away in time to keep him from seeing the tears in her eyes.

He sucked in a breath.

Layne never cried.

He waited till she disappeared through the doorway with the kids. He checked the counter area to make sure Shay had stayed in the back room. And then he shoved his bowl away from him and slumped back in his seat.

How had this all gotten so complicated?

Before he'd come to town, his plan was simply to check up on his child and convince Layne to take the child support he owed. Now, it looked like he'd have to prove himself to her. But how could he do that?

He'd run into plenty of skepticism from folks in town already and knew he would face more—and worse— once he encountered Layne's brother. At the rate he was going, he'd have to prove himself to the whole of Cowboy Creek.

Both of which might be easier to handle than facing Layne.

With her, he'd gone beyond just the need to prove himself a better man. Now, according to the challenge she'd thrown at him, he had to earn her trust again.

He *wanted* to do that.

But, given their history, getting her to trust him could be a downright impossible goal.

Chapter Nine

Layne had just finished settling Jill in her crib when she heard a faraway rapping on the apartment door. Her thoughts shot to Jason.

When they had arrived home from the Big Dipper, he'd escorted them into the apartment. The minute he had set Jill's carrier on the couch, he'd announced he had errands to run. That was the last she had seen of him all afternoon.

When he got back, she would bite her tongue till it bled rather than admit she missed him. And yet she did, more than she wanted to admit even to herself.

She had left Scott playing with his cars in the living room. As she came down the hall, she heard him run to the apartment door and call out.

"Who is that?"

"Hey, Scott. It's Grandpa Jed."

Frowning, she crossed the room. She and Cole had always looked to Jed Garland almost as a substitute father. But, though she often saw him at SugarPie's and at parties and barbecues out at the Hitching Post, she couldn't remember the last time he had come to the apartment. As she swung open the door, she half expected to see

Jason beside the older man. Instead, Jed stood alone, his white hair rumpled and his Stetson in one hand.

"Come in." She stepped back. "Is everything okay? It's not something with Cole? Or Tina and the baby?"

"No, no, nothing like that." He stepped into the room. "For one thing, Sugar said you were under the weather. I thought I'd drop by and see how you're doing."

"Better, thanks. Much better."

He glanced past her. "Jason not around?"

"No. Uh…he had a few things to do. Can I get you a cup of coffee? Or tea?"

He waved the offers away. "Don't want to put you out."

"You won't be. I was just going to heat up the kettle for tea for myself."

"The same will be fine for me, then."

She went toward the kitchen, leaving Jed to seat himself in the armchair she had begun to think of as Jason's. The thought made her wince. She *was* getting too used to having him around…a problem she might not have to worry about for much longer.

Her hands shook as she took the tea canister down from the shelf. A delayed reaction from the walk, that was all. Their stroll to the Big Dipper and back again had worn her out. So had the strain of her conversation with Jason and the uncomfortable near-silence on their trip back home.

She filled the kettle, assembled mugs and spoons and dessert plates, arranged gingerbread cookies in a shallow bowl, all without paying attention to what she did. Her mind wasn't anywhere near her actions in the kitchen.

She only hoped Jason's errands hadn't included going straight to Jed. Why he would do that, she didn't know, but Jed's arrival seemed much too coincidental. If all was well with Cole and Tina, what other reason would he have to stop by?

And where was Jason? It was getting close to supper time. To her dismay, she realized she had been stalling, holding off on deciding what to make for herself and Scott, expecting Jason to walk in the door at any minute.

Maybe he didn't plan to come back. Maybe he had left town again.

Maybe that was what had brought Jed here today.

She knew one thing for certain. Standing here in the kitchen worrying over all these questions wouldn't get her any answers.

In the living room again, she set the serving tray on the coffee table and handed Jed a mug.

"Cookie, Mommy?" Scott asked.

"Just one. We'll be having supper in a little while." She looked at Jed, who sat back in his chair and sipped his hot tea. He didn't seem to want to launch into conversation—which put her even more on edge. Jed always had something to say. She forced herself to make small talk, postponing the moment she would find out why he was really here. "How is everyone out at the ranch? I haven't spoken to anyone since I got sick. Except Shay. She told me the wedding was beautiful."

"Everybody's just fine, and the wedding went off without a hitch."

Despite her tension, she laughed. Since the Garlands had begun holding weddings at the Hitching Post again, that had become Jed's favorite phrase.

"More to the point," he said, "how are you?"

"Much better, as I said. I think the flu is on the way out."

"And how are things going now Jason's back again?"

She took a cookie and set it on a dessert plate, then settled against the couch with the plate on her knee. "I don't know what you mean by 'back,'" she said slowly. "He helped me out with the kids when I wasn't feeling well, but he's gone now."

"Not from Cowboy Creek. And I've got a hunch he's not going anywhere soon."

"Why do you say that?"

"Well, he came back here for a reason, didn't he? And as proud as I am of the Hitching Post, I doubt he returned just to soak up the ambience of the surroundings there, like the saying goes." He looked at her over the rim of his mug. "Though he hasn't said as much, I'm willing to bet his trip's got to do with you. And your boy."

She glanced quickly at Scott, who had finished his cookie and returned to playing with his cars. "He wanted to see Scott," she admitted in a quiet tone.

"That's not a bad thing, is it?"

I want to make up for lost time, he had told her. "He said he wants to help me. By giving me child support, not by staying around and building a relationship with... with Scott."

"Maybe he thinks he wouldn't be welcome."

"Did he say that?" she asked. "Did he ask you to put in a good word for him with me?"

"Not at all. I'm here on *your* behalf, girl. And if that includes talking him up, then so be it. Shay says he's been staying here, watching out for you and the kids. Sounds to me like that's a help to you and a step in the right direction for him."

"A step too little, too late." Even as she said the words, she flushed, thinking of all Jason had done for her in the past few days. And all they had both said in their argument at the Big Dipper.

"If that's what you've set your mind to, that's what you'll tend to believe. It doesn't mean it's the truth. But my point is, you can't handle everything on your own, especially when you're recovering from the flu. Whether or not he's laid out his thoughts about the future, he's proven his good intentions for now, hasn't he?"

She stared down at her mug.

"Layne," he said gently, "whatever happened between you two, whatever might be going to happen, he *is* your boy's father, after all."

For all the contact you've had with him, you could have been a sperm donor.

She winced and gripped her mug. "On paper, Jed, but not the way it counts."

"No. Not legally, since you two never went that route. But morally, now that's a different story."

She heard the heavy footsteps out in the hallway then a knock at the door.

Scott scrambled to his feet. To her dismay he had learned to recognize that quick-tap, too. "Jason's home!" he yelled.

She almost choked on the lump in her throat. What would happen when Jason left "home" again…for good?

She set her mug and plate on the coffee table and went to open the door. He stood in the hallway, his arms crossed and legs planted as if he might never leave the spot again. But as she pulled the door wide, he stepped inside.

He caught sight of Jed, and his brows rose in surprise. Either he hadn't sent the other man here, or he'd just done a good job of faking his reaction. "Hey, Jed."

"Wondered when you'd get back. After I left Sugar-Pie's, I moseyed over here to see how Layne was doing." Jed set down his mug and rose. "It's past time for me to get back out to the ranch."

"About that room you're holding for me—" Jason said.

"Ah. Well. That's the other reason I stopped by. Tina called me while I was still at Sugar's. My boys and their wives decided to stay on a couple of days, and we've had some new guests check in. I'm afraid we haven't got a single room to spare. But I'd reckon that's not a problem. Layne's put you up for a few nights now, and I'm sure she can handle one or two more. Can't you, Layne?"

She looked at Jed, who stood smiling at her.

Then she made the mistake of looking at Jason. He had raised one eyebrow the way he had always done after issuing a challenge he expected her to refuse.

So she did what she had always done. "Of course I can handle it," she said defiantly.

SOMEHOW, SHE AND Jason had managed to eat supper and straighten up the kitchen, then spend the evening in the living room with Scott, all without incident... until Sugar called.

Layne had answered the phone in the living room, where Jason and Scott sat on the floor with the toy cars spread out around them. She noticed Jason reaching for the remote. When he muted the television, she had felt grateful for not having to strain to hear over the canned laugher. In the background while she spoke to Sugar, Scott made occasional engine noises as he raced his cars down the runway.

By the time she hung up, she wished Jason had left

the sound on to prevent him and Scott from hearing her end of the conversation. Worse, she had begun fighting the uncomfortable feeling he had muted the program only so he could listen in on her call.

It was horrible of her to think that, but how could she doubt it when the first words out of his mouth related directly to what she had said to Sugar?

"How do you expect to go back to the shop and put in a full day on your feet?" he asked.

"I'll be fine."

"You mean, you'll be stubborn as usual. You were still tossing your cookies two days ago," he reminded her. "And don't try to pretend you weren't worn-out after the walk this afternoon."

"I'll bounce back." But she knew in her heart—and her weak legs—she still wasn't up to caring for both kids and working a full-time schedule.

"Sugar doesn't want you back yet," he said flatly.

"You listened to my conversation?"

"I figured if you didn't want me to hear, you would have gone into the other room." He grinned. "I guess it pays to be careful what you say around adults, too."

"Very funny. And yes, she told me to stay home for another day."

"Sounds sensible to me. You've got to see things from her perspective. She can't have an employee passing out on the job. Or worse, serving up germs to all her customers."

"I know that," she muttered. "But I need to work."

With one hand, he effortlessly boosted himself from the floor and settled onto the cushion beside hers.

"Show-off." She stiffened and pressed her back into the couch, hoping to get some distance. But he turned her way and leaned closer, obviously trying to catch her gaze. She raised her chin and stared back at him.

Which was definitely not a good idea.

He was so close. Too close. For the first time since seeing him again, she allowed herself to actually *look* at him. To take in his dark eyebrows, his slightly crooked nose, his lush dark lashes. And his eyes. Those caramel-brown eyes with darker brown flecks that once upon a time had held her mesmerized.

They held her captive now. She couldn't break eye contact. Couldn't blink. Couldn't breathe.

"Oops!" Scott said.

Jason turned his head.

Freed, she took a shuddering breath and let it out again.

Jason knelt down to readjust the cardboard runway. By the time he returned to his seat, she had regained control. She had also shifted position, sitting sideways with her legs crossed and hastily pulling the afghan from the back of the couch to cover herself with, creating both distance and barriers between them.

Coward, a little voice in her head whispered.

No. Better to be safe than seduced—by my own imagination.

He rested his arm along the back of the couch, leaving his fingertips still too close to her shoulder. She had nowhere else to go, short of getting up from her seat and moving to the chair or finding an excuse to leave the room. Instead, she stood her ground...so to speak.

"Listen," he said quietly, "regardless of how much you think I've done for you, you've given me food and a place to sleep and a shower. If you're keeping score, I'd say that makes us even. You can stop worrying about paying me back. But I doubt you'll stop worrying over your bills. We haven't worked out a deal for child support yet—"

As she opened her mouth, he rested his hand on hers to forestall her. Warmth spread through her as if her fever had spiked again.

"Maybe we never will agree on that," he continued. "But at least let me advance you something to get you through."

She shook her head. "I'll keep Scott and Jill home for a few more days. That will save on the babysitter."

"And then you can't work, so how will you handle the bills?"

She sighed.

"Layne. If you don't want to take the money for yourself, think of your kids. I have no problem with helping you for their sakes."

She pressed her lips together, tugged on the edge of the afghan, laced her fingers through the open weave. There were more knots in her life right now than in this afghan Tina's grandmother had crocheted for her.

They had a full pantry and refrigerator again, thanks to Jason, though she hadn't wanted to accept his help with her groceries. She didn't want to accept his money now.

He is *your boy's father, after all*, Jed had reminded her.

For their sakes, Jason said.

She couldn't default on her credit cards or be late on the rent.

She couldn't let her kids suffer for a decision she had made years ago.

And she wouldn't let it seem as though Jason showed more concern for her own children than she did.

"I don't want Cole to hear anything about this," she said slowly. "He doesn't know I'm struggling…just a bit…financially. He has a little boy of his own and a baby on the way, and I don't want him even thinking about helping me."

"He sure won't hear it from me."

She stared past him for a few moments, watching Scott on his knees running his cars up the ramp Jason had made. His head was bent over his play. Jason's eyes stayed focused on her.

"All right," she said at last. "I'll…accept your offer. As a loan."

"We'll discuss that angle another time."

"Jason, help."

At Scott's plea, he looked away, turning his attention to her son, giving her another moment to herself. She sagged back against the couch and exhaled heavily, hoping she hadn't just sold her soul to her ex.

There were bound to be catches to this arrangement, complications she couldn't foresee. But what was done was done. Resolutely, she sat up again. "Since you're here for another night, I'll get you a proper pillow and some bedding. I didn't mean for you to go without them all this time." She flushed. "I guess I was too out of it to think about that before."

"No worries. I slept in the chair, anyhow."

"You didn't. Every night?"

He shrugged. "It's a comfortable chair."

"Like a *truck*?" Scott asked.

He laughed. "Even better."

"Speaking of sleeping, honey," she said to Scott, "it's time for little boys to be in bed."

"No. Wanna play cars with Jason."

"I think you want to listen to your mama," he said.

"Read me story?" Scott held up his arms.

"I can do that."

Before she could say anything, Jason had scooped him up and set him on his shoulder. He brought her son over to her and leaned down so she could give Scott a kiss. She wanted to protest. But Jason had handled bedtime for the past few days now. How could she tell Scott Jason couldn't read to him tonight?

Worse, what was she going to face when she had to tell Scott Jason wasn't there to tuck him in? The thought made her heart hurt, both for her son and for herself. It made her wonder if she wasn't protesting the events unfolding around her nearly as strongly as she should.

She swallowed hard and kissed her son's cheek. "You behave and go to sleep for...for Jason. You hear me?"

Scott nodded.

Heart in her throat, she watched them cross the living room. Jason ducked down to clear the doorway. Scott laughed and scrunched his fingers in Jason's hair.

When they disappeared from view, she sat staring at the empty doorway, her thoughts shifting to another apartment very much like this one.

So many nights, she had run her fingers through Jason's hair, too, feeling the contradictory crisp yet smooth sensation against her palms, inhaling the scent of his aftershave, tasting the salt of his skin as she kissed his shoulder.

She rubbed her palms across her eyes to blot out the memories.

They were too much to think about.

This entire situation was too much, too family-like, too special. Too close to the life she had expected to have with Jason.

WHEN JASON ENTERED the kitchen a while later, Layne turned to look at him. She had just run some water in the kettle. Raising her eyebrows in question, she held up the kettle, catching his attention.

"Yeah," he said. As she ran more water, he went to the cupboard and took down a couple of mugs, then reached up to the shelf for the tea canister.

It was as if he'd always lived here with them. As if they were a team.

Suddenly, she wondered what *she* would face when he wasn't there to tuck Scott in. The thought made her shiver. Maybe she should have put her foot down and read tonight's bedtime story.

"Cold again?"

"No."

He rubbed her upper arm as if to warm her. Instead, his touch only sent a series of shivers racing through her. He tilted his head, giving her no option but to meet his gaze. "Having the chills this bad has to mean something."

If he only knew.

"I just haven't shaken off this flu yet." She sidestepped him and went to the refrigerator for the milk pitcher.

At the stove, the kettle began to whistle. He poured their mugs and set them on the table, then took his usual seat. She settled in her chair and stared down at her mug.

"I knew you weren't up to speed," he said. "You probably ought to hit the hay as soon as you've had your tea."

A vision of them together in her bed flashed before her eyes. She blinked it away. Why was she responding to him like this? He had already been here for days, and she hadn't had a reaction.

Her fib about the flu gave her an inkling of the truth. While she'd been down and out, the flu must have suppressed her hormones. But there was nothing stopping them from working at full strength now.

"You need to move to the Hitching Post," she said abruptly.

He looked at her in surprise.

"I mean, you can't keep sleeping in a chair. And my couch won't be any better. It was too short for Cole when he used it, so it will certainly be too short for you."

"Trying to kick me out?"

"No." But she could feel the telltale flush spreading up her neck and over her jawline.

"Layne."

She tensed. "What?" He had used the tone she recognized from years ago. The one meant to convince her of something. To sway her to his point of view. To win an argument.

"Jed said there might not be a room for a day or two. I hope you plan to let me bunk down here till then."

"Do I have a choice?" she said irritably. "All right, fine. But I hope you don't plan to spend all your time in the apartment."

"In or out of it, I want to spend the time with Scott."

And *there* was the first catch to letting him stay. The first complication she hadn't foreseen—but should have figured out long before this. Could she blame her dull wits on her flu symptoms, too?

Feigning a calm she didn't feel, she sat back and sipped her steaming tea.

"You're keeping him home from day care," he reminded her in the same tone.

"What does that have to do with anything?" But she knew his answer before he said it.

"He'll be around and so will I."

But for how long?

She sighed. She had agreed to take financial help from the man. The obligation already weighed her down. She didn't need to let that force her into anything else. Even so, she knew the situation had turned into something more.

She wanted the best for both her kids. What mother wouldn't? Yet Jill's father ignored her existence, just as Jason had ignored Scott's…till now. She couldn't deny her son time with a daddy who wanted to see him—no matter how short a time that interest would last.

"You can't be with him every minute," she said slowly. "I don't want him getting any more used to having you around than he's gotten already."

He shrugged. "I'll find something to keep me occupied for part of the day."

"And I don't want you alone with him, either."

His jaw set and his lips thinned as if he were fighting to hold back his response. For a moment she thought he would refuse to accept her terms. But finally, he nodded.

"All right, then," she said. "You can see Scott, as long as I'm there with you."

To her dismay, she realized *that* was the second complication her muddled brain had let her get tangled up in. She had just negotiated a deal that would force her to spend more time with Jason.

Chapter Ten

The early-morning sun blazed through the kitchen blinds, making Layne's eyes water. Yawning, she covered her mouth with the back of her hand.

"Tired?" Jason asked.

She blinked. He had been standing at the refrigerator with his back to her. She hadn't realized he had turned in time to catch her midyawn. "A little," she told him.

A lot, she confessed to herself. Between Jill's midnight feeding and her own restlessness, she had barely gotten any sleep.

"I could take Scott off your hands for a while this morning," he said as he poured orange juice into a plastic cup. He fit the cover in place with a crisp snap.

"Nice try," she snapped almost as briskly, trying to keep from glaring at him. At her tone, Scott looked up from his coloring book. She smiled at him and stroked his hair. As he returned his attention to his book, she gave Jason a level stare over her son's head.

Was he going to force the issue on their agreement already? Was this her chance to call their verbal contract null and void? And wasn't that what she wanted? Yet, why did all those questions make her heart thump, and not in a good way?

When Scott held up the coloring book to show Jason, she had her answer. Her son and his daddy had formed a bond that Jason's departure would break.

"Nice job, buddy." He set the cup of juice on the table at Scott's elbow and looked at her. "If it's not too early to run the washer, how about we throw in that load of clothes you talked about?"

"I can take care of it later this afternoon."

"I'm out of clean socks."

"Oh." If that was what he needed to be on his way, she would have run a load with a solitary pair of socks—because *she* needed him to be on his way, at least for a while. She needed time to think. "All right. We can start the machine now."

While he went to the living room for his bag, she crossed the kitchen. That morning, she had deposited a half-filled basket of the kids' clothes on the floor near the closet. After she finished loading detergent into the machine, she turned back for the basket—and nearly collided with Jason.

He stood bare-chested in front of her, the shirt he had been wearing dangling from his hand, a pile of other clothes held in one arm. A scattering of dark hair covered his chest. Below, hard abs and a narrow waist drew her gaze downward to the worn-soft waistband of his jeans. The sight left her heart pounding. A jolt of memory stole her breath.

"I just saw I'm out of T-shirts, too," he said.

Mouth dry, she nodded, snatching the shirt from his hand and taking the pile of clothing from him. After tossing everything into the washer, she closed the lid and tried for a steadying breath. Then she edged a half step away from him. "I'll get you one of my sleep shirts. They're just plain T's, extra-large."

"Thanks."

She nodded again and left the room, trying not to look as if she were on the run. But she hurried down the hall at double-speed, one hand flapping near her face to cool herself. No worries about chills now. No way.

The only thought in her mind at this moment centered on what else the man had in his duffel bag.

If he discovered he was out of clean underwear, she was in big trouble.

JASON KILLED A couple of hours and a half tank of gas roaming the outlying roads around Cowboy Creek.

He passed ranches where he'd once thought he might settle in as a wrangler, and eventually he slowed the pickup to a crawl when he neared the gates of Garland Ranch.

He didn't want to go chasing Jed down so soon when he'd just seen the man the day before. And he sure didn't want to barge in on the man's family and friends, all of them hanging around to visit after the wedding...and one of them, at least, sleeping in the room meant to be his.

No matter. Layne's couch had suited him just fine.

Last night, he'd have taken the armchair again without a word of protest, if need be. He tried not to think what that meant.

He didn't want to go back to Layne's at the moment, either. He checked the dashboard clock. Eleven fifteen. It had been a while since breakfast and was close enough to lunchtime to look for something to eat. The snack bar inside the Bowl-a-Rama opened early.

Back in town, he pulled into the parking lot of the

bowling alley and slammed the driver's door shut as if
he could slam a lid on his memories of what had happened in Layne's kitchen.

The sedan he had parked near sported the bumper
sticker: My Grandchild's an A+ Student at Cowboy
Creek Elementary.

He laughed derisively. No one would catch *his* grandmother with that sticker, or his mother, for that matter—
even if he'd gotten the grades to earn it.

Lack of interest more than lack of brainpower had
made him slack off in classes when he should've been
applying himself. He and Layne had already been a couple long before high school, but it wasn't till then that
he'd started walking that fine line between pass and fail.
She had tried to help, and he'd eagerly signed on for their
study sessions. But his enthusiasm had nothing to do
with the homework assignments. Still, he'd left school
with a diploma in his hand.

Scott was a bright kid. With luck, he'd take after
Layne with her interest in learning and do well in school.

Inside the Bowl-a-Rama, he went directly to the
Lucky Strike. The snack bar was overlaid with the familiar scents of frying grease, coffee left on the burner
too long and bowling shoes that had been worn by too
many feet. Behind the counter stood a man wrapped in
a once-white bibbed apron already streaked with grease
and ketchup.

"You still slinging burgers here, Mel?" He rested his
crossed arms on the edge of the counter.

The older man squinted at him, then shook his head.
"Jason McAndry. Jed told me you were back in town."

What else had the man said? Was everyone in Cowboy Creek now aware he'd come back? Were they talk-

ing about his shortcomings and blaming him for the way he'd left Layne? "And I don't just sling burgers," Melvin was saying. "I own the place now. So, what are you up to these days, chasing the girls or the bulls?"

He laughed. "Both. Every chance I get."

"Then what the hell you doing in Cowboy Creek?"

The smile slid from his face. "What are you talking about?"

"Layne. That's *who* I'm talking about. She's the only girl in town you ever chased. She brings her boy in once in a while on half-price days, if she's got time off from SugarPie's. That's more than anybody sees you doing."

Damn. He gritted his teeth. Sugar Conway and Shay O'Neill and now good old Mel. What kind of story had Layne told the folks in this town?

Then again, the true story was bad enough. And after four years of skating on his responsibilities, he should have expected everyone to rally around Layne.

"You want something from the grill?" Melvin asked.

"Burger. With fries. And a large sweet tea." He'd already been condemned. He ought to be entitled to a last meal.

Melvin turned away. Jason took a deep breath.

Earlier that morning, he had made a quick stop at the sandwich shop for a fresh doughnut and a coffee to go. At that hour, he'd known Sugar would be tied up with the bakery half of the business and unlikely to step foot in the adjoining shop. Not that he would have run from a confrontation with the woman, if it had come to one.

No, it was thoughts of Layne he was trying to outrun. Thoughts of how she'd taken one look at him with his shirt off and hightailed it out of the kitchen and down the hall. Thoughts of how hard he'd struggled to keep from following her down that hall and into her bedroom.

He needed some time away from her. Some distance from the familiar look in her eyes and the flush in her cheeks and especially from the hitch in her breath that had always revealed what she was thinking.

Things he'd been thinking much too often, lately, too.

But he had to keep his focus on his goal. He needed to earn her trust, not find his way back into her bed—no matter how enticing that idea had become.

Melvin set a tray with the tea he'd ordered on the counter in front of him. "I remember the days you two used to come in here. Other than the fights, you looked like a sure bet to me. I'd'a thought you both coulda worked things out."

He wasn't the only one who'd thought that. "Yeah... well, I guess you'd have gotten it wrong." His first taste of the tea was sweet, cold and unsatisfying.

With a flourish, Melvin slid the paper plate containing his burger and fries onto the tray. "Then I'll say what else I'm thinking, and I'm not wrong about this. Your mama's long gone from town and I don't know why else you'd come back, unless it has to do with Layne. That girl's got lots of friends here, and they'll be watching out for her."

"They already are," he confirmed. He nodded his goodbye and found a table at the far end of the snack area. The burger was just the way he liked it, hot and loaded with ketchup, and yet as unsatisfying as the tea.

He could blame that more on Melvin's attitude— and Sugar's and Shay's and Layne's—than on the food and drink. But he had to be honest. His dissatisfaction stemmed from a whole other source.

When he'd woken up that morning, he hadn't intended to leave Layne's apartment. He had planned to stick to his guns and spend the time with Scott, regardless of the part-time and supervised arrangement she'd forced him to agree to. Yet, as soon as her dryer had spit out his load of clothes, he had done some hightailing of his own.

He'd put space between them—just what she had looked for all along. She wanted the kids to herself. Or at least, not near him.

It still burned him to know Layne wouldn't let him see Scott on his own. All right, he hadn't talked to the boy until this week. But despite what she'd said at the Big Dipper, surely considering the days he'd spent with her and the kids, he ought to have earned some level of her trust.

That looked to be a long shot since even the whole danged town seemed unwilling to give him any benefit of the doubt.

The longer he stayed here, the more he was coming to realize folks had cause for thinking the way they did. Still, he'd hang in there and keep trying. Because he wanted to earn Layne's trust—and more.

He wanted her to forgive him for what he had done.

AFTER LUNCH, LAYNE and Scott had just put their jackets on to go for a walk when Jason turned up again. While he'd been gone that morning, Scott had asked about him several times. She had assured him Jason would come back. In a way, she might have been reassuring herself. She couldn't bear the thought of him treating her son the way he had treated her—walking away and then staying away for years.

Overjoyed to see Jason, Scott demanded he go along

with them. In turn, Jason insisted on pushing Jill's carriage. She knew when she was outnumbered. Besides, their matching stubborn expressions nearly broke her heart.

"We seem to be establishing a routine," she said to him as they left the apartment. She wasn't sure how she felt about that.

"Routines are for old folks," he said. "Isn't that what we always used to say?"

"Old married folks," she said, trying to hide her dismay at his offhand reminder of their past. Back then, she had imagined them staying together and becoming that long-married pair. She had always thought he wanted that, too.

"Go to the park?" Scott asked.

"Not today," Jason said flatly.

Prepared to give that same answer, she had already opened her mouth. She snapped her jaw closed again. His expressionless tone had been more of a giveaway than if he had stressed the words. He was thinking about her unwillingness to let him take Scott to the park on his own.

Maybe the opportunity to be with their son had meant more to Jason than she had thought. She wasn't sure how she felt about that, either. And yet she couldn't deny how much it bothered her that he refused to go the park with them as a…as a group.

When they reached the corner, Jason turned in the opposite direction.

The sun was hot on her head and shoulders, making her overly warm in her jacket. Reluctantly she admitted to herself she was glad he'd taken the reins of the carriage…so to speak. She felt stronger than she had the day before, but she certainly wasn't up to running a marathon. Or even pushing a baby carriage for more than a few hundred yards.

They walked for a while in silence, except for Scott's occasional questions. Eventually, they turned down a street of A-framed houses with small yards in front.

"You used to live down this street, didn't you?" she asked. She had never visited Jason at home. He hadn't come to her house much, either, for that matter. They would hang out at SugarPie's or the Big Dipper. Less often, they would meet at the library, where she would try to coax him into studying while trying to resist his plans of stealing kisses in the book stacks.

She had met his mother and her boyfriend shortly before she and Jason were married and had only seen the woman a few times after that. Once he left town, their brief connection ended abruptly, too.

"It's the blue one at the end," he muttered.

They walked slowly down the block. The house before Jason's was painted lemon yellow with white woodwork and lacy wooden trim along the edge of the porch roof. It looked like a house from one of Scott's storybooks. The woman who stood sweeping the porch looked like a storybook character herself, with her wire-rimmed glasses, soft white hair arranged in a bun and a calico apron worn over a pale blue cardigan. She saw them, waved and smiled. "Hello, Layne," she called. "And Scotty."

"Hi, Mrs. Browley," she said.

"I heard you weren't feeling well, you poor thing. Why don't you come on in and sit for a while? I've got cookies fresh out of the oven. They won't hold a candle to Sugar's, I know, but a chocolate chip is a chocolate chip any day, I always say."

"Cookies, Mommy! *Please?*"

Smiling, Layne nodded at Scott. "Thanks, Mrs. Browley. We'd love to stop in."

"I'll leave the door open and go put the kettle on." She set her broom against the porch railing and went into the house.

"Mrs. Browley is a regular at SugarPie's," Layne said quietly to Jason as he turned the carriage up the front walk. "She's also very lonely, I think. Her husband died about five years ago. But you would know that, since she was your next-door neighbor."

"Yeah. Mrs. B and her husband were always good people." He said the words almost grudgingly.

"She still is." They followed the sound of the older woman's voice down the short hallway to the kitchen in the rear of the house.

"I hope you don't mind if we have our tea party in here. It'll save us carrying everything out to the parlor. If you'll just help me shift this table, young man—" She cut herself off and stared. "Why, Jason McAndry, is that really you?"

"Yes, ma'am, it is." As if he felt uncomfortable under her scrutiny, he turned away to hook his Stetson on one of the kitchen chairs.

"Well, what a nice surprise. Let's get this table out from against the wall and we can sit down and have a real chat."

The kettle began to whistle. Without a word, he rearranged her kitchen set to accommodate them all around the small table. Layne removed Jill's blanket and assisted Scott with his jacket.

After they were seated with steaming mugs of tea in front of them and a heaping platter of cookies in the center of the table, Mrs. Browley said, "This *is* a treat, having you all here. And you're saving *me* from having to eat every one of these cookies myself. I would, too." She laughed. "It's lovely having you visiting again, Jason. I'm afraid your mother never did say where you'd gone when you left…"

The half question hung in the air. Layne wondered whether or not he would answer. He still seemed uncomfortable. She couldn't imagine why, when no one could be less threatening than grandmotherly Mrs. Browley.

"Texas," he said finally. "I've got a job wrangling at a ranch out near Dallas and spend the rest of my time competing in rodeos."

"Well, that's just wonderful. My husband used to say rodeo was dangerous work but nice if you can win in it."

Jason smiled. "That's true."

"And do you win?"

He shrugged. "My share."

He said it so casually, and yet years ago, it was exactly because he *didn't* win in it that they had faced their biggest problems. Rodeo was an expensive sport, especially when you didn't have sponsors or bring home the biggest purses. And when it took you away from the full-time job and you had bills to pay and a baby on the way.

"I haven't heard a word from your mother since she left, either," Mrs. Browley said. "She and Lou broke up, and a good thing, too, though of course, that's not for me to say." She glanced at Scott, who was busy devouring a cookie, and lowered her voice. "The yelling and carrying on that went on in that house, it was pitiful." She shook her head. "As sorry as I was to see you move on,

Jason, I think in the long run it was better for you than moving back home."

Maybe that was why Jason had never taken her to his house. For the first time, she understood his home life might have been almost as bad as hers. Yet he had shouldered his troubles without saying a word, all the while listening to her, making more of an effort to support her than she had realized.

"But don't mind me," Mrs. Browley went on. "I'm just talking out of school. My husband used to say I had so many opinions about people in this town, I should have run for mayor."

"You'd be a good candidate, I'm sure," Layne said warmly.

Beside her, Jason reached for a cookie and sat munching it while she and Mrs. Browley—or primarily Mrs. Browley—carried the conversation.

When the platter was cleared off down to the last crumb, the older woman beamed. "I'm just going to go right ahead and send the rest of the cookies home with you. I can bake another batch later. And you're all welcome to come by again anytime for more."

"Tomorrow?" Scott said.

At that, even Jason laughed.

"I don't know about tomorrow," Layne told Scott. "But we'll definitely stop by to say hello again sometime."

"Good enough," Mrs. Browley said. "Now I know to expect company, I'll make sure to keep the cookie jar filled."

As they left Mrs. Browley waving goodbye to them from the porch, Layne glanced toward the blue house next door. But when they reached the sidewalk, Jason turned the carriage resolutely in the other direction as if he didn't want to walk past his former home. Or didn't want to revive any more memories.

Chapter Eleven

When they arrived home again, Jason and Scott immediately settled down in the living room.

"I'm taking this little girl in for a change," Layne told them. But once she lay Jill in the crib, the baby began to squirm, pursing her lips and turning her head toward the mattress. "Uh-oh. Mommy knows those signs. Somebody wants to eat."

Tired from their walk, Layne curled up on Scott's bed and held Jill close.

The afternoon with the four of them together had eased some of her tension. To her surprise, she had begun to feel comfortable with having Jason around the kids. Unfortunately, she was also beginning to feel much too comfortable with him herself.

He had things on his mind he wasn't sharing with her, but he didn't need to tell her so. Just as with Jill's hunger, she could read his unspoken signs. She wanted to know why he'd been so quiet at Mrs. Browley's.

Jill finished nursing, and Layne held the baby upright, lightly patting her back. She heard Jason's boot steps in the hall. A moment later, he stood framed in the doorway. Jill let out a loud burp, and they both laughed.

"What are you feeding that kid—beer?"

"Now, that's one thing she's never tasted." He stepped into the room. Whatever tension had eased inside her immediately snapped to attention again.

"She ready to go down for her nap?"

She nodded. When he reached out, she hesitated for only a moment before letting him take the baby. She watched as he carefully cradled Jill in his big hands.

"That's right," he murmured to her, "time for you to hit the hay."

Layne blinked and had to tear her gaze from them.

This was what their lives would be like if they could have made their relationship work. The thought filled her with warmth at the same time it left her breathless, battling too many thoughts to take in at once.

Over this past week, almost without her being aware of it, moments like these had become normal parts of their day. Feelings she hadn't expected—good and bad— had taken root inside her. A longing to be with Jason again. Her worry the problems between them were her fault. The growing fear she had driven him away.

But she couldn't allow herself to believe that. It took two to make a marriage work.

She watched him settle her daughter in her crib and thought of all her son had missed. All *she* had missed.

Her eyes blurred and she blinked, but not fast enough to hold back a tear. Quickly she brushed it away. She couldn't let Jason see her breaking down just because he'd put Jill in her crib. But he turned around and caught her with her hand on her cheek, and to her dismay, another tear fell.

He came to sit beside her and reached up to wipe the moisture away. "Don't," he said. He lingered, brushing his thumb across her cheek and tucking his fingers beneath her chin.

"I can't help it. I…"

"I know." He tilted his head to rest his chin against her hair.

She could smell his aftershave, his shampoo, the soap she kept in the shower. The good clean scents she had always associated with him. For a moment, she felt tempted to lean against him, simply to get close to him, the way Scott and Jill cuddled against her. A basic instinct born of the need to touch, to be touched. To connect without words.

As if he felt the same, he leaned back and looked down at her. He lifted her chin and stared at her mouth and then, slowly, raised his eyes to meet hers. Her heart tripped a beat, and she knew she was losing that heart to him all over again.

Silently, he lowered his head. She tilted her face up to his. She felt the brush of his breath against her lips, a welcome caress. She felt the heat of his mouth just an inch away…

The heat warned her, reminding her how quickly their kisses could go from a gentle warmth to a raging fire.

She shook her head, breaking away from the contact she longed for. Trying not to think of the closeness she craved. "No. What if Scott walked in? We're sending him enough mixed messages as it is."

"You're sending me a few, too."

She shivered. She wasn't the only one who could read signals and, this close, he hadn't missed hers. "That was always the issue, wasn't it?"

But now, she was confused by the messages she was sending herself. Seeing Jason with the kids, doing the things daddies do, made her long to believe he could be the husband she had always wanted.

But she had tried that once…

Twice…

How could she know *what* she wanted in a husband? She couldn't trust herself to pick the right man—*any* man—to fill that role.

She scooted to the other side of the bed and stood.

"What was that about 'the issue'?" he asked.

"Our problem," she clarified. "We had always been good at…going wild and crazy. But when it came to everything else, we couldn't handle it. And a relationship built on wild and crazy isn't a relationship at all."

She turned her back to him. He said nothing else. She leaned over the crib and, with one finger, stroked Jill's cheek.

Behind her, she heard his boots hit the floor as he left the room.

She touched her daughter's hand. Jill's tiny fingers tightened around hers. The connection coursed through her, creating a wave of pure love.

Her thoughts jumbled inside her head again, triggering a wave of complete panic.

What was she doing getting so close to Jason, coming so close to kissing him, doubting so many of the decisions she had made? Hadn't she learned her lesson yet? How could she risk hurting her kids by falling—again—for a man she couldn't trust?

LAYNE CURLED UP on the couch in the living room, now lit only by a single table lamp. Jason had gone to read Scott his bedtime story and tuck him in.

A few minutes later, he joined her.

Each night, he had begun emptying the contents of his pockets—his key ring, his wallet, his money clip—into the drawer of the coffee table. She envisioned him instead using the bedside table in her bedroom. Imagined him sharing her bed...

Would she never stop having thoughts like those about him?

Swallowing a sigh, she shifted on the couch.

They had made dinner and cleaned up afterward without a single word about what had happened—or not happened—in the kids' bedroom. Everything had seemed normal. Familiar. Routine.

As if they were just a couple of old married folks.

He reached for the remote. "I'll keep this turned down so you can hear the kids."

"Thanks."

More thoughts tumbled inside her head. More questions. If he'd been around from the time Scott was born, would he always have been this considerate? Or in the space of those three years, had he matured as much as she had? Could she take the risk of finding out?

The TV droned on, the murmur occasionally punctuated by a noisier commercial or a laugh track as he flipped through the stations. The flickering of the screen against the surrounding dimness made her squint. In the background, the dishwasher in the kitchen made a rhythmic hum. Her eyelids felt as if she'd balanced a weight on them.

"Hey, Layne." Dimly, she heard his voice. "Hey, Layne," he said again softly. "Time for bed, don't you think?"

She had fallen asleep. Yawning, she stretched her arms over her head. When she saw he sat watching her, she self-consciously lowered her hands to twine her fingers together in her lap. "The baby will be up for a feeding before too long. I would be better off trying to stay awake."

"How 'bout a game of cards, then?"

"Cards?"

"Yeah. Gin rummy, a penny a point, like the old days."

"I don't think so. I haven't played cards in forever."

"What do you do with yourself after the kids go to bed?"

"Read a magazine. Watch television. Throw in a load of laundry. We run out of clean socks, too." Instantly, she envisioned him standing in front of her with his shirt in his hand. She regretted the words as soon as she'd said them, but he simply laughed, making her feel better about her misguided attempt to keep things light.

"I'll bet." He changed position in the chair to face her more comfortably. "Don't you ever leave the kids with a sitter and have a night on the town?"

"Oh, right. Like the old days?" she repeated mockingly. "The highlights of our high-school years? Live it up at the Bowl-a-Rama and then hit the Big Dipper or SugarPie's a half hour before closing?"

"They were fun days."

She nodded. "And you were always all about the fun."

"Me? Most of the time you were the one who didn't want to go home."

To her surprise, she realized he was right.

"Sugar had to kick you out."

"Sometimes." Reluctantly, she admitted, "It was better to be out of the house than dealing with my dad." She had told him what it was like for her at home, with neither of her parents paying her or Cole much attention, except when her dad found something to complain about or criticize.

"Yeah," he said, "when I first met you, I thought you were lucky. At least you had two parents."

"Trust me," she said drily, "anyone seeing us at home would never have known we had even *one*. I don't know what I'd have done without Cole." She had been open with Jason about her family situation. To a point. He had always been closed up tight about his. Their hostess's conversation at the tea party that afternoon had given her information about his mother's relationship that she had never known. "I didn't realize your mom and her boyfriend had split up. Where did she go? As Mrs. Browley said, she moved away from Cowboy Creek not long after you did."

"Yeah." Not looking at her, he reached for one of Scott's storybooks on the coffee table and sat riffling the pages. "She got fed up with Lou and went to stay with one of her sisters in Albuquerque."

"How is she doing?"

He shrugged. "I left a couple of messages not long after. When she finally called me back, she made it plain she had a new life with a new guy and it didn't include having a grown-up son."

"Oh, Jason. I'm sorry." Rejection from a distance had to hurt less than being ignored by someone who sat in the same room with you. But it wouldn't help him to hear that. She hesitated, then said, "In all the years I've known you, you've never talked about your dad."

"There was nothing to say. I never had one."

"Never?"

"Not one I ever saw."

"Did…did he die?"

"Nope. My mother got fed up with him, too, I guess. It was just me and her, until she hooked up with Lou and he moved us here to Cowboy Creek." He glanced at the television again. His profile in the flickering light looked hard-jawed and grim.

His admission bothered her. From the time she had met him, she knew his father wasn't in the picture, but she hadn't known Jason had never seen the man.

Though she would be the first to attest he might not have missed much, no one could really say for sure. Just as she could never know what it would have been like for her son to grow up having a father at home.

But now, she certainly couldn't miss these clues Jason had given her. Even if he'd wanted to, he might not have known how to be a daddy.

THE MINUTE JASON walked into SugarPie's late the next morning, he saw Layne's attention zero in on him. Her face took on the familiar blank expression she used to hide her surprise, but the widening of her blue eyes gave her away.

She should have known he would come by to pick her up at the end of her shift.

This close to lunchtime, the booths in the back had filled. He slid into a chair at a small round table off to one side of the room. From there, he could see her a few tables down, taking an order from an elderly couple, probably there early for the lunchtime special.

It was her first day back to work, and that morning, he'd insisted on driving her to take the kids to the sitter and then dropping her at the sandwich shop. "I've got nothing else to do but kill time," he had argued, "and it'll save you gas money."

"Normally I walk."

"Not today," he'd countered, and her lack of argument proved to him her energy levels weren't back to normal. The way she'd tossed and turned in her bed for yet another night told him how much being sick from the flu and having a brand-new baby must have messed up her sleep schedule. He'd heard her movements again because—no matter the relative comfort of the short couch over the armchair—he'd been up half the night himself.

Notepad and pencil in hand, she made her way to his table. "What can I get you?"

"Into trouble?" He grinned.

"We'd done enough of that a long time ago." She waggled the notepad impatiently.

"I'll wait for you."

"I won't have time to eat here. Since Sugar wouldn't let me put in a full shift, I told Rhea I'd pick the kids up as soon as I finish at noon."

"And while you went to get the baby settled in the playpen, I told Rhea it'd be closer to one."

She gasped. "You *what*?"

"Don't worry. I'll take care of paying her for the extra time."

"Jason," she hissed, "that's not the point. You can't rearrange my life to suit yours."

"I did it for *you*. After being on your feet all morning, you'll need a break and something to eat. To fortify you before you have to deal with the kids again."

Her mouth opened, then closed, as if she didn't trust herself to speak. Again, her eyes gave her away. She blinked several times, and he'd wager she was trying to hold back tears. For a moment, his gut clenched. He sure didn't want her crying here. The night before in the kids' room, she had shed a couple tears and they had nearly done him in. The two of them had almost started that trouble he'd jokingly mentioned just now—though last night, he had felt no urge at all to laugh.

When he'd wiped the moisture from her cheek, she had jumped away from him the way a greenhorn shied from a skittish horse. That was about the only thing that had stopped him from leaning closer and stealing a kiss. But if she cried now, he wouldn't be able to keep himself from wiping away her tears.

He could just envision her reaction if he dared to do that in the middle of SugarPie's.

"I'll bring you a sweet tea," she mumbled. Abruptly, she turned away.

Over near the cash register, he saw Sugar handing change to a customer. She had her gaze trained on him. If she thought he was upsetting Layne, she wouldn't hesitate to come and show him the way to the door.

A minute later, Layne brought his tea and a straw. "You sure you don't want to go ahead and order?"

He shook his head.

"Fine. Here's a menu to keep you occupied. I'll be off shift in another half hour or so."

He didn't need the menu when he could sit back and enjoy the view as she walked away. She wore a pink headband that matched her shirt and held her hair away from her face. The long, golden-brown strands fell in waves down her back. Her hair smelled like wildflowers. He knew this from the lingering scent of her shampoo when he'd taken his shower after she had finished hers. He knew this from resting his chin against her hair last night.

Last night, when he'd come within a millimeter of kissing her.

He'd had thoughts in that direction before then, and he'd had to struggle not to give in. He wanted her. And it wasn't just about sex.

The more time they spent together, the more humbled he was to see how much she loved her daughter and his son. The longer they were together, the more amazed he was to see everything she handled as a single mom, from grocery shopping with both kids in tow, to carting them halfway across town to the sitter and then trekking back again on her own to get to work. And with every day that went by he caught more glimpses of the girl he had loved.

He grabbed his tea glass and took a gulp, trying to distract himself from his own thoughts. As if he didn't already know her feelings, Layne had made them perfectly clear. A relationship between them wouldn't stand a chance.

Sugar came bearing down on him from across the room. With the coast clear, she must have decided to close in. She took the extra chair at his table. "What's the verdict?"

The abrupt delivery combined with her soft accent threw him. "About what?"

"About Layne holding up for the rest of her shift. The way you were eyeing her up and down, I assumed you were checking to make sure she would last the morning."

"I was just looking around."

"Oh? I didn't see your gaze wandering to my pastry case, and that's what usually catches folks' attention."

"Don't worry, I checked that out when I walked in. I hear you cater the sweets for the receptions at the Hitching Post. I may check with Jed to see if they want to branch out. Mrs. Browley makes a mean chocolate-chip cookie."

Sugar gave a snort that made him think of Burning Sage, who'd come so close to head-butting him at the rodeo in Cheyenne. Funny, until the conversation with Mrs. B, he hadn't given a thought to rodeo since he'd gotten back here. For sure, Greg would have something to say about that.

Sugar leaned forward and said in a low voice, "You won't know the definition of the word *mean* if you do wrong by Layne again." Rising, she said with a smile, "Enjoy your sweet tea."

"And my lunch. Layne's joining me after she finishes up."

"That's nice. So long as you're footing the bill."

He laughed, letting her have the last word. She meant well. They *all* meant well.

Sobering, he looked down at his glass of tea. He knew now just how wrong he'd been years ago. These past few days had shown him how much he had lost out on as a result of his own actions, how much he had missed by not being around for Scott's birth. He was grateful for this chance to see his son now.

But this short visit wasn't enough. He'd already come to the conclusion a week here and there wouldn't satisfy him, either. He wanted the right to see his son anytime he could.

He shot a glance at Sugar as she made her retreat.

Despite what anybody in this town believed, this time around, he was determined to do the right thing.

Chapter Twelve

Layne ate her small salad and cup of vegetable soup as quickly as she could without seeming as though she were shoveling food into her mouth. She couldn't help noticing the sidelong looks she and Jason were receiving. There hadn't been this much excitement in SugarPie's since the day six-year-old Tommy Engleson had let his pet lizard loose. Accidentally, of course.

Jason had chosen a small round table that, with his long legs, put them knee-to-knee. She was conscious of each time his jeans brushed her panty hose and every time his boots hit the toes of her work shoes.

"Sorry," he muttered after yet another collision.

She wondered if he had picked the table because it would put them this close together. She also wondered what he and Sugar had been so cozily discussing and laughing about earlier.

Not that she was paranoid. Or that she was trying to manufacture reasons to get upset with him. But between Sugar and Jed and Mitch and anyone else he might have spoken to since his return, she couldn't help wondering something else. Maybe he was trying to get back into their friends' good graces—by making her out as the bad guy. By showing them what a nice guy he was.

When Sugar came by to drop off the check, he snagged it from her fingers.

"I'll take care of it," Layne protested.

"Too late." He rose and went to the cash register.

Smiling complacently, Sugar followed him.

Layne slipped into her jacket and went to wait near the door.

No matter what he was trying to show people, she couldn't deny he *was* a nice guy, especially when it came to the kids. He never turned down requests to color with Scott or to play with his race cars or read to him from his storybooks. He didn't ignore her daughter to spend time only with their son.

Though he'd drawn the line at volunteering his diaper-changing services again—a thought that, despite everything, made her fight a smile—he had gotten over his initial awkwardness around the baby and grown more comfortable with handling her. He would settle Jill in her crib, shake one of her small rattles to get her attention, or return her pacifier to her mouth. And when he talked to her, his tone was different from the one he used with Scott. He seemed to have learned to adapt to the kids' personalities.

She wished she and Jason could adapt their personalities to one another, too.

He tucked his wallet into his jeans and approached her, giving her a smile that lit his eyes and made her knees weak. "Ready?"

She nodded. She said goodbye to Sugar and a couple of the regulars seated near the front of the shop. Jason held open the door for her.

The day had turned overcast, and there was now a chill in the air, accompanied by a stiff breeze.

"*Brr-r-r.* Looks like we might be in for some bad weather." She crossed her arms and headed for his truck. When he matched her stride and casually draped his arm around her shoulders, she almost missed a step.

"Looks like for once, the forecasters were right," he said. "They predicted some rain."

"You mean, *for once*, you actually slowed down to notice what was on the channel?"

"I've been noticing a lot of things lately."

"Oh?" She kept her gaze on his truck and tried to keep her tone light. "Like what?"

"Like Jill's got your chin, and she sleeps in the same curled-up position you do."

His response surprised her, but she couldn't have appreciated anything more than a comment about one of her kids. She smiled up at him. "Yes, she does."

"And like Scott's got your blue eyes and the same stick-to-itiveness when it comes to getting something done."

"He is pretty focused sometimes." She stopped beside the truck and waited for him to unlock the passenger door. He kept his arm wrapped around her shoulders. Her heart started to thump.

"And like you still fit up against me as if we were two puzzle pieces linked together."

"We're a puzzle, all right," she murmured.

He moved to stand in front of her. He reached for the lapels of her jacket, holding them closed, protecting her from the breeze. "I always did enjoy a good puzzle." He tugged gently, bringing her a shade closer as he dipped his head.

His mouth was cold from the air around them, minty from the plastic-wrapped candy he'd taken from the dish beside the cash register. She wondered if he'd done that deliberately, too, taken the mint with the knowledge he intended to kiss her. The thought that he might have wanted…might have planned…might have looked forward to just this moment sent a pleasurable thrill racing through her.

"Still cold?" he murmured against her mouth. He slid both arms around her, holding her against him, warming every inch of her, outside and in.

They stood in the parking lot, in public, in view of her friends, the way they had done all over town during their dating days, and somehow she didn't care. She let him kiss her, and she kissed him, too.

And she wished they could go back to those days and start all over again.

JED SAT BACK in his office chair and propped his feet on the corner of the desk, his ankles crossed. From that angle, he had a clear sight line to the two women who sat on his small couch. They had a strong resemblance to one another, his granddaughter young and dark-haired, his cook with her once-dark hair now streaked with gray. Neither one of them looked happy. And if his womenfolk weren't happy, he was bound to hear about it. "Well, there's no sense sitting there with your mouths locked tight. From the long faces you're giving me, I know something's up."

Tina and Paz exchanged a glance.

"Things are not so good in some parts of the Hitching Post, Abuelo," Tina said.

He locked his fingers across his belly and waited.

"Cole knows Jason's back in town," she explained.

"So you let the cat out of the bag, huh?"

"Jed," Paz said reproachfully. "You can't expect her to keep secrets from him. Cole is Tina's husband."

"More important to this conversation," Tina said, "he's Layne's big brother."

He shook his head. "And I can just imagine how he took the news. But it wasn't a secret, it was just postponing the inevitable. The boy didn't need the distraction while he's running the ranch for Pete."

Paz let out a definite snort of disbelief, and Tina laughed outright.

"Well, all right," he conceded, "so I wanted him out of the picture for a bit. We knew he'd find out one way or the other. Now we just need to make sure he doesn't gum up the works. Sugar says Jason and Layne are doing fine—with a little extra lovin' care from her, as she calls it."

"That's a good thing," Tina said. "Right now, she and Shay are our best bets for finding out what's going on in town."

"Oh, I've got plenty of folks keeping an eye on that pair," Jed said smugly. "Shay and a couple of the others phoned in to tell me Jason and Layne had lunch at SugarPie's. And that's not all. You should have heard what those two got up to in the parking lot, Paz. Kissing. While standing right there for all the world to see."

Her eyes rounded in surprise.

Tina slumped back against the couch and heaved a relieved sigh. "Well, I'm so glad to hear that. For a while, I was wondering if we were on the right track."

"We are, for sure. Just standing in the wrong station. Sugar and Shay and everybody else are fine for helping out. But we—you and me, ladies—have got to do something to hurry things along." He thought for a moment.

"This working from a distance has me roped and tied. It's time to get the pair of them out here to the ranch."

"What's the hurry?" Tina asked. "Is Jason planning to leave again soon?"

He shrugged. "Who knows? But he might get it into his head to do just that. And if it's anything like the first time he left, nobody will know a thing until he's long gone."

JASON DROVE AROUND and behind the Hitching Post to park near the barn and the corral. To his surprise, he had the parking area almost all to himself. The hotel guests might have gone off to see the sights—though there weren't many sights to see unless you went all the way to Santa Fe.

He would have stopped in to greet Jed's ranch manager but knew Pete wasn't yet back from his honeymoon.

After their lunch at SugarPie's, he had taken Layne to pick up the kids at their day care, then dropped them all off at her apartment. Following the terms of their agreement, since he'd been on his own that morning, he could have stayed. Could have spent time with Scott.

But after his time with Layne in SugarPie's parking lot, he'd felt the need for some space.

A couple of hotel guests were braving the cooler air to take instruction in the proper way to mount a horse. Then again, if they were from up north, at this time of year they probably found New Mexico a tropical paradise compared to back home.

He scanned the corral, expecting to see Cole Slater, but the cowboys giving the instructions were strangers to him.

Gripping the steering wheel, he stared over the hood

of the truck, seeing not the corral but Layne's face when he had kissed her.

The way she returned his kiss proved she was feeling the same things he was. Didn't it?

But even if his own conscience hadn't started nudging at him, reminding him of how badly he'd once treated her, his encounters with some of the folks in Cowboy Creek wouldn't let him forget. He'd had to pull away from her. He had to stick to the promise he had made to himself. He wasn't giving in to any kind of attraction, getting caught up in any kind of "trouble" with her. Not until he had proven himself.

As if he could shut his thoughts into the pickup truck, he slammed the driver's door closed and headed toward the hotel. A man came down the back steps and strode toward the parking area, his hat brim shading his face. Not a guest on the ranch, but one of Jed's wranglers. One of his grandsons by marriage. Layne's brother, Cole.

He paused and waited for the other man to approach him. They'd been on civil terms once upon a time—for the most part anyway. But after all the years that had passed since then, he couldn't expect that now. Besides, Mitch Weston had warned him Cole would be ready to give him an earful when they met. Better to see the man here and get this confrontation over with, rather than face him inside the hotel and make things awkward for everyone, especially Layne when she learned about it.

And knowing the folks in Cowboy Creek, she would learn about it.

Cole stopped in front of him. "I heard you were back in town."

"I heard you were managing the ranch."

"Temporarily, while Pete's away."

He nodded. "Jed tells me he keeps a full stable, the way he always did. Daffodil still around?" He'd had a soft spot for Daffodil, a mare Jed had pulled from the herd, claiming she had earned her keep and an easy retirement.

"Yeah, she'll never leave the place. Unlike some cowhands I know."

"You also know the hands come and go."

"And some don't come back for a good long time. Until it suits them, I guess."

He scowled. "I'm not the only one of us who left town and took a while to come back. Or so I hear. Besides, your sister threw me out."

Cole raised his brows and spread his hands in disbelief. "What was the difference between that time and all the others? You two broke up more often than I've broken in a new saddle. Though I have to say I thought it was all over between you when you dumped her on her sixteenth birthday. That was low, considering she was still getting over losing our mama. But no, like always, you got together again. Until you left for good. What kind of man does that?"

"I told you, she kicked me out. I knew she had you to depend on. How could I know you wouldn't set foot in Cowboy Creek again for a while, either? But she had Sugar. Jed and Tina. Other friends. It's not like I left her all on her own."

"No, you sure as hell didn't. You left her carrying your baby. A man doesn't walk away from a woman he's gotten pregnant. Not knowingly. I told Layne if I had suspected that would happen, I'd never have signed the paperwork to let the pair of you get married."

"It takes two to make a pair."

"You forgot the rest of it, pal," Cole said. "It takes two people willing to stick around and work things out. Is that what you've got in mind now? Because if you start something with her again without having any plans to stay, you won't have a chance of steering clear of me. You've already messed with Layne's head—you and Terry both. And I'll break your neck before I let you break her heart again."

Cole strode past him.

He stood with his hands fisted, taking a few deep breaths. From behind him, he heard the roar of an engine. He stood and watched as Cole drove away.

Damn the man, but he was right.

What was he trying to prove by rekindling a relationship with Layne? What was the point in trying to earn her trust? Except for his son, Cowboy Creek now held nothing for him but reminders of why he had stayed on the move. As soon as he could come to terms with Layne about child support and a visitation schedule, he was only going to leave town. He was only going to hurt her again.

He turned back to his truck, but before he'd reached it, he heard someone hailing him from near the hotel. Jed had come out onto the back porch.

After a final deep breath, he made his way in that direction.

The older man stood waiting for him, his thumbs hooked in his belt loops and a smile on his face. "Well, what brings you out here this afternoon?"

"Coffee would do, for starters."

"C'mon in, then. You've picked a good time. Let's head around to the front and go through to the dining room. The place'll be quiet. I'd invite you into the kitchen to say hi to Paz, but it would be more than our lives are worth for me to step foot in there with you now. She's halfway between lunch cleanup and supper prep."

Jed led the way through the empty hotel lobby and hung a right down the hall to the dining room. "I was going to get in touch with you today anyhow. Paz and Tina have invited you for Sunday dinner. I imagine you remember well enough not to cross Paz when she wants to serve you a meal."

"You've got that right." He laughed and shook his head. "I missed a couple of suppers she invited me to, and I thought I'd never hear the end of it."

"Well, cooking for folks is her way of showing she cares." Jed gestured to a carafe on a side table. "Maria just put out a fresh pot of coffee. Help yourself."

He poured a cup and took a seat at the smaller table near the window Jed had chosen.

"If you're looking for Cole, you're out of luck. The boys found a break in a water pipe out by one of the supply cabins, and he's gone into town to pick up what they'll need to take care of things. He left only a bit ago. In fact, I'm surprised you two didn't pass each other along the road."

"We met out back just now." Jed's brows went up, maybe in question, but as far as he was concerned, the less said about that conversation, the better. "I'm not looking for anyone in particular, just killing time." He didn't know why he'd driven out here at all, except, like the apartment he'd once shared with Layne, he had always felt comfortable at the Hitching Post. The cup of coffee had only been the first excuse to come to mind.

"Killing time?" Jed said. "That doesn't sound good."

He shrugged. "Layne went to work for a while earlier today. She said she's doing okay, and she's sticking around the apartment this afternoon."

Jed eyed him for a long moment, then said, "I don't guess it was easy for her, having you show up again out of the blue."

"I suppose not."

"No supposing about it. You've got to keep an open mind about how she's thinking."

"I'm trying to. But that ought to work both ways."

"Sometimes it's hard to let your guard down, especially when you've got good reason to put it up in the first place." When he said nothing, Jed sighed and went on. "Son, you're on your own, you can come and go as you please, can make decisions without having to consider anyone else's welfare. Layne has got more than just herself to think about."

"Yeah. I know that."

Just as he knew what he'd done to her was wrong. He'd already acknowledged it and wanted to make amends. And naturally, Layne had dug in her heels and fought him.

The grief he was getting from folks didn't make that easy, either.

He really hadn't had a clue what his return to Cowboy Creek would be like. But he sure couldn't miss the challenges now.

Chapter Thirteen

"How is everything going with Jason?" Shay asked.

She had arrived on the doorstep so soon after he had left, Layne almost wondered if her friend had been keeping the apartment under surveillance. But that was a crazy thought.

All through their conversation, Shay hadn't once mentioned Jason's name—until now, just when she had slipped into her jacket and was getting ready to leave, too. Just when Layne thought she might have managed to escape having to discuss her ex…her *first* ex.

Could Shay have waited deliberately, wanting to catch her off guard?

Another crazy thought. What was wrong with her? When she had met Shay at the L-G Store, she had misunderstood her friend's concern. And now she was letting her uncertainty over Jason make her read too much into everything. Shay was a good friend, one she could trust.

With a sigh, she rested against the armchair Jason favored. "Everything's perfectly fine. When it's not absolutely awful."

Shay laughed and settled onto the couch again. "Now, that was the most contradictory answer I've ever heard. So, which is it? Tell me the truth."

She glanced across the room. Scott was playing quietly—so far—while Jill napped in her playpen. She looked back at Shay. "The truth is, I don't know how things are going. Jason is…he seems to be getting along with the kids. And for Scott's sake, I have to want that."

"And for your sake? What do *you* want?"

"Just that. I guess." She smacked the arm of the chair in frustration but kept her voice low. "Shay, I'm the *last* person to know what's best for anyone, including myself. Once, I thought I wanted Jason. I thought we wanted each other. And you see what happened there. Then I thought things would work out with Terry. But that didn't go as planned, either."

"You can't count that. The two of you weren't together more than a few months." Shay hesitated, then added, "Don't get upset, but…did you ever think you might have picked him up on the rebound?"

She blinked. "No," she said slowly. "That never occurred to me. But maybe I did. If so, unfortunately, that would only help prove my point about not knowing what's best. After all, what kind of mother would do that to her child?"

"You're a great mom. And you were only trying to give your son a daddy."

"I wish I could convince myself that's all it was." But she knew in her heart it was so much more.

As she walked Shay to the door, she heard footsteps out in the hallway, followed by a brisk knock at the door.

When she opened the door, her brother, Cole, gave her a smile. It looked genuine, but nothing like the wide grin she was used to from him. She didn't recall the tiny frown lines in his forehead, either.

"Hey, stranger." He spotted Shay behind her. "Well,

look who's here. I run into you at the Hitching Post more often than I see my sister at all."

"And I'm going to run right now," Shay said, "so you can spend lots of time with her." On her way out of the apartment, she waved goodbye to Layne. "I'll call you."

At the sound of Cole's voice, Scott had rushed to the door. Layne watched while Cole caught him up in a bear hug and ruffled his hair.

"Uncle Cole, look." He led Cole by the hand across the living room to show him his new motorway. "For my cars."

"Hey, that's not bad, Scotty. I'll have to get Aunt Tina to bring Robbie over here sometime. You like to play cars with Robbie, don't you?"

Scott nodded emphatically. "*And* Jason."

Layne's heart sank. She had hoped that somehow—by some form of magic, maybe?—they would get through Cole's visit without Jason's name coming up. But that hadn't worked with Shay. And now the look Cole shot her said it was a worthless hope with him, too.

"What are you doing here on a workday?" she asked. She pushed away the thought he had made the trip in from Garland Ranch just to talk about her ex-husband. Then again, Cole knew he could talk to her about anything at any time. It didn't always mean she felt prepared with answers. "Can I get you something? Coffee? Pop? Something to eat?"

"Sweet tea, if you've got it. Be back in a few minutes, Scott." He followed her into the kitchen, then settled into the chair Jason always used. He glanced at the extra place mat without commenting on it. "I had to make a run to the hardware store and thought I'd drop by while

I'm in town. With Pete away, I may not get the chance for another week or two."

"I was so sorry to miss the wedding. Shay told me everything was wonderful."

"Sure, if you call another man down being wonderful."

She laughed. "Oh, stop. Pete's a lucky man. And you know getting married was the best thing you've ever done."

"Well…" Now he gave her his usual grin. "I can't argue with you there. And you can't argue with me about this—supper at the Hitching Post Sunday night. Tina and Paz are having fits since you didn't make it to the wedding and they haven't seen you in so long. They both made me promise I wouldn't come back to the ranch without getting you to agree. And if I fail and they kick me out, I'd have nowhere to go."

She laughed. "I'd always have room for you. You know that."

"Not right now, considering you've already got a houseguest."

She walked to the refrigerator for the tea pitcher. "No worries about where you'd go anyhow, since the kids and I would love to come for supper."

"Good."

"How's Tina doing?" she asked. She poured a glass of tea and hoped she had successfully changed the subject.

"She's fine. Worried about you and your flu right now."

"I'm fine, too."

"I'm more worried about the lingering aftereffects."

Her hand trembled just a bit as she set his glass of tea in front of him. Unfortunately, she knew that had nothing to do with the flu. She sank into her seat across from him. "Except for feeling worn out, I'm doing okay."

"That's not what I meant."

"That's what I was afraid of."

"When you opened the door, you and Shay looked like you'd been in a serious discussion," he said quietly. "And I'll bet I don't need two guesses to figure out the topic. Are you sure you know what you're doing, letting Jason stay with you?"

Her laugh sounded a little crazed. "Right now, I don't know anything about *anything*. But Jed said you had no rooms open at the Hitching Post, and I couldn't just kick him out."

He hesitated for a moment, staring at her, his eyes the same shade of blue as Scott's and her own. Finally, he shrugged. "We could've put him up in the bunkhouse."

"He was a big help here when I was sick, I have to admit that."

"And what now?"

"I don't know. He wants to spend time with Scott."

"And that's it?"

"And," she added reluctantly, "he wants to pay me child support."

"Why shouldn't he? I never did get why you wouldn't take it from him—and go after Terry for it—in the first place. You're entitled to the support, and so are the kids."

"I know that. But I'm getting by." And she *was*. Yes, she sometimes worried about making ends meet, but by the end of the month, she succeeded in paying her bills. If she hadn't been hit by the flu, she would have managed this month, too.

"It's their daddies' obligations to take care of them," Cole insisted. "You wouldn't have wanted me not to do my best for Tina and Robbie if things didn't work out with us, would you?"

"No, of course not. But you're different, Cole. You're such a great husband and daddy, a wonderful man, in spite of everything you had thrown at you when we were growing up. You would never have walked away…"

"The way Jason did."

She nodded.

He swore under his breath. "You know my feelings on that. I can't tell you enough times, if I'd've known how things would work out with you two, I'd never have signed the okay for you to get married."

"It wasn't your fault. And I can't even blame everything on Jason. Maybe we just weren't meant to be." That was only one of the worries she had tried to block out of her mind as she tossed and turned half the night.

She was falling for Jason again, with no guarantee that, even if they did renew their relationship, it wouldn't end the same way it had the first time. "But what if *none* of it was Jason's fault? What if it was all mine, and I drove him away in the first place?"

"Is that the bull he's been feeding you?"

"No. It's what I'm feeling. Not one but two marriages down the drain. What does that say? Obviously, that I'm not cut out for wedded bliss. Maybe I'm not cut out for any kind of relationship at all. I think about Mom and especially about Dad and all the things he used to say and—"

"Stop right there. You can't waste time worrying about those things."

"I didn't before, but after Jason, and then Terry… I think about those things now. And maybe I even believe them. I've never had a relationship work out—"

"That's not all on you. And this isn't just about making a marriage work, is it?" He took her hand. "You would never tell Scott or Jill they weren't worth loving, would you?"

Just the thought made tears spring to her eyes. "Of course not."

"Well, then, you can't believe that about yourself. You know I love Robbie more than anything, and I feel the same about the baby we're having, sight unseen. Unconditionally. No strings attached. Just the way you feel about Scott and Jill. And that's the way you need to feel about yourself."

She wanted to believe him, but there were too many memories to fight.

As if he understood, he squeezed her hand. "Layne, you need to forget the past. Stop worrying about what happened before and focus on what's ahead."

She wanted to believe him about that, too. But at this point, she couldn't imagine what her future might hold. Except for supper Sunday night at the Hitching Post.

Visiting Garland Ranch would give her something to distract her from her thoughts. And, thank heaven, it would finally give her what she desperately needed—a break from Jason.

If he hadn't already left Cowboy Creek by then.

LAYNE REACHED FOR the drying towel and took a plate from the rack. After dinner, Jason had insisted it was his turn to wash dishes.

"Most of the hands in the bunkhouse hate cleaning up after meals," he said, hanging the dishcloth on its hook. "I always like when it's my turn to wash, because when you're done, you're done."

"Lucky you."

He grinned. "Well, next time we'll draw straws. How about that? Because I *am* done here." He looked over at her son, who sat at the table, coloring. "So, c'mon, Scott, let's go. I've got a surprise for you."

Her son slid from his chair. "Yes-s-s. *Es-s-s,*" he chanted. "Surprise for Scott—*surprise!*"

Jason laughed, and they left the room together.

With the kitchen so small, she didn't have to move more than a half step from the counter to see directly into the living room. She didn't know where Jason had gone that afternoon, but he had come home with a small plastic sack he'd left on the end table near his chair. He grabbed it now and rummaged inside, then pulled something from it.

"Coloring books!" Scott exclaimed. "C'mon. Let's color."

She smiled and stood for a moment, watching them.

As she dried the rest of the dishes and put them away, she occasionally peeked through the doorway. Jason sat on the floor with Scott on his knees beside him. They both leaned over the coffee table, working together.

She hung her drying cloth on its hook. Pausing, she looked at the dishcloth hanging beside it and thought about what Jason had said.

Next time we'll draw straws.

As if there *would* be a next time. As if they had a chance. As if he had plans to stay. Or did he mean to drop in only occasionally, when Scott would have to get to know him all over again and then have to live through losing him one more time? Would she have to face that heartbreak again, too?

Swallowing a sigh, she straightened her spine. She was the mom here, and she had to protect her kids.

When she entered the living room, Scott immediately looked up and held out his crayon. "Color, Mommy."

She nodded. "Okay. I'll take this book." She went to reach for a second coloring book.

He shook his head. "No, Mommy help. *Please*." He smacked his hand flat on the page he'd been working on. The page opposite the one Jason sat coloring.

Even if she could have thought of a reason to say no to Scott, she knew she wouldn't have turned him down. Such a simple request. What could it hurt—even if it meant sitting elbow-to-elbow to share a coloring book with Jason. She took the crayon and settled on the floor beside him.

"He's very enthusiastic about coloring," he said mildly.

She couldn't help but laugh. "That's an understatement." She held up the crayon Scott had given her. It was still large enough for his small hand, but so worn down there almost wasn't enough left for her to grip.

"Ah," Jason said. "Well, I think I can take care of that. I brought a surprise for you, too."

"Surprise for *Mommy*?" Scott asked in amazement.

"Yep." He reached into the plastic sack and pulled out a fresh box of crayons. "Maybe she'll let you use them, too, Scott."

She laughed. "Of course, I will."

"Surprise for *Jill*?" Scott asked expectantly.

"Oh, honey," she rushed in, wanting to save Scott from disappointment. And, strangely, *not* wanting to see Jason's discomfort because he had thought only of her son and not her daughter. "The coloring books and crayons—"

"—are for Mommy and Scott," Jason finished. "And of course there's a surprise for Jill." He reached into the sack again, this time pulling out a small, plastic-wrapped teething ring.

She stared down at the picture Scott had been "coloring" until the bright scrawls of color seemed to melt and run before her eyes. Blinking to clear her vision, she picked up a worn crayon. She couldn't risk a glance at Jason at that moment. Instead, she looked at the package he still held, the gift he'd bought for a little girl who wasn't his.

Despite every concern she had about him, how could she not lose her heart to this man?

"For Jill." Scott reached for the package.

"She's sleeping now," Jason told him. "We can give this to her in the morning. How about you put the surprise on the table in the kitchen?"

"Okay." Scott headed across the room.

"Thank you," she said. "It was nice of you to think of the kids."

"I was thinking of you, too," he murmured. He reached for her hand and smoothed his thumb across her knuckles. "Didn't want you getting cramps in those fingers."

She laughed, knowing immediately what he meant, and it wasn't only a reference to Scott's crayon stubs.

She and Jason had joined the decorations committee for the eighth-grade winter festival—he reluctantly, to gain extra credit for their English class, and she ecstatically, as soon as she heard he would be on the committee, too. "I don't think my fingers have ever recovered from cutting up all those snowflakes."

"Guess I should have taken my turn, the way I do at the dishes, and not left all my snowflakes for you."

"Yes, you should have," she agreed. She pulled her hand to free her fingers, but he didn't let go.

Instead, he tightened his grip slightly and leaned closer. "Guess I owe you an apology."

"Yes, I guess you do."

He rested his free hand on the back of her neck. Heat seemed to spiral down her back to the end of her spine. He slid his fingertips into her hair at her nape. A tingle ran all through her. A smile creased the corners of his eyes, telling her he knew just what he had done.

Holding her steady, he bent his head, taking her mouth with his as if he had never been away. He knew just how she liked to be kissed and just where this would lead to…if they had been alone.

She heard Scott's footsteps as he ran back to the living room. She broke away from Jason, turning from his wide-eyed look of surprise and catching the same expression mirrored on her son's face.

Chapter Fourteen

Curled up on the couch, Layne watched Scott, who knelt at the coffee table beside her. His arrival had averted what could have been a disaster. Another few moments alone with Jason, and who knew what might have happened to her resistance. Who knew what might have happened that she would regret.

She didn't want to think about how swept up in the moment she had been.

In the awkward seconds after she had broken away from him, she had been glad for the distraction of Scott and his coloring books.

Jason, seeming almost as uncomfortable as she felt, excused himself to take his shower. She firmly refused to let her mind go there.

She had been unsettled enough by his kisses.

"Mommy kiss," Scott said.

She started, wondering if she had said her thought aloud. Smiling, she leaned down to press her lips against his hair.

"No." He shook his head and gestured to the couch. "Mommy kiss Jason."

She felt herself flush to the roots of her own hair. "Yes, Mommy kissed Jason." And Jason kissed Mommy thoroughly enough to curl her toes. "But not anymore, honey." She promised herself that.

As if her answer satisfied him, Scott went back to his coloring. She lay against the couch cushion and closed her eyes, unable to resist the images that came to her of Jason in the shower.

After a while…a long while…she was able to push those images aside.

Indulging in visions like those and exchanging kisses with Jason would complicate an already unbearable situation. It would only put her heart in more danger.

Worst of all, it would only make things harder for her son. Jason might not have to consider what was best for Scott, but taking care of her children was the number-one priority on her list.

Opening her eyes, she sat up again, determined not to let anything shake her resolve to keep her distance from Jason…and his kisses.

Evidently, Scott had lost interest in the coloring book and opened the drawer in the coffee table. Jason's key ring sat in a jumble on the book's open pages. Beside the book lay his wallet. Scott had strewn credit cards and cash across the tabletop.

"Oh, honey. Those are Jason's." She began gathering the cards. "You're not supposed to touch—"

A folded piece of paper caught her eye.

A piece of paper she recognized because she had a duplicate of it. She couldn't have made a mistake. The sheet was yellowed with age and folded into a small rectangle, but on one corner, she saw part of a headline from Cowboy Creek's local paper, an article on a new store that had opened in town three years ago.

And on the back…

She unfolded the paper. Afraid her trembling hands might accidentally tear the well-creased edges, she lay the paper in her lap. Open, it revealed the local birth announcements from the day her son was born. She had a copy of one of those announcements, carefully cut from the newspaper, pasted into his baby book.

Tears welled in her eyes and trickled down her cheeks. She sat frozen, unable even to wipe away the tears, stunned at the knowledge Jason must have carried this announcement in his wallet for all these years.

And yet he had never come back to see Scott, never sent a birthday card or a Christmas gift. Never acknowledged he had a son—except for those envelopes that had come with nothing but checks inside. After ripping up the first couple of checks, she had returned the later envelopes unopened.

And now he wanted to give her child support. More money that would come with no emotional attachment and no commitments.

How could that unfeeling man be the same one who cared enough to carry her son's birth announcement in his wallet?

JASON TUCKED THE blanket around Scott and set the stuffed panda and teddy bears on either side of him. He turned on the night-light on the small dresser beside the crib. Jill had curled up with one fist under her chin. Just like her mama. Smiling, he turned back to Scott.

"'Night," the boy mumbled in the middle of a yawn.

"'Night…" he echoed.

Good night, son, he wanted to say instead.

Good night, Daddy, he wanted to hear Scott say in return.

It was too soon for that. Layne wasn't ready yet to accept child support without giving him an argument, let alone allow him to tell his son the truth.

But maybe she was ready for something else. Judging by her reaction to his kiss, she wouldn't say no to another one. If not for Scott running into the living room and interrupting, at that point, she might not have said no to anything.

At the moment, he'd settle for another kiss. For a step in the right direction.

Eagerly, he headed back to the living room.

Layne had moved to the couch. She sat with her arms around her upraised knees, the afghan pulled across her, looking less like a woman who wanted to be kissed than any he'd ever seen.

He'd have to make a detour and hope that was the right way, too.

He took the seat beside her. "Need a tuck? I'm getting pretty good at them, if I do say so myself."

"No, I'm fine."

"When I left the room, Scott was about ready to nod out. Jill curled into sleep position the minute I set her in the crib." He lay his hand on her knee and plucked at the afghan. "We know where she gets that from."

"It's a habit of mine," she agreed.

"Scott..." He hesitated. No, she wasn't ready—and truthfully, *he* wasn't ready, either—to approach the subject of telling their son he was his daddy. They'd get to that in time. But for now, they had other things to talk about. Finally, he said, "I can see where Scott takes after you, too. He loves his books, and Rhea says he loves the lessons she teaches."

"He does. And I try to reinforce the basics he's learning there."

"That's my Layne," he said, keeping it light. "Looks like you've had better luck with him than you ever had with me."

"He pays attention," she said just as lightly, but her smile seemed strained.

"It's more than reinforcement," he continued. "Rhea told me he's learning a lot here at home, too. He knows his alphabet, which is more than she could say about the other kids his age."

"Thanks." Her cheeks flushed with pride.

He wanted to say how proud he was of Scott, too, but knew better than to attempt it. "I bet you'll have one of those 'my kid's an A-plus student' bumper stickers on your car the minute he gets into grade school."

"I probably will."

"That's good to hear." Again, he hesitated, then went on. "Does he have any of my habits?"

She tilted her head and narrowed her eyes. He counted off the seconds, knowing she was deliberately making him wait. "Well, he's obstinate when he wants something and cranky when he doesn't get his way."

"Very funny."

"I'm not laughing." But a smile tugged at her lips. "He's very focused when he wants to be. And he's outgoing. You know he gets that more from you than me."

"He favors me, too." He almost subconsciously straightened his shoulders as another wave of pride filled him. "When I look at him, I see the kid I used to be."

"So do I," she said softly.

"That's good to hear, too." He edged closer, leaning against her upright knees. "Now, where were we before I went to read Scott his bedtime story? I seem to remember..."

She remembered, too. Her eyes drifted closed in a signal he understood well—anticipation, acceptance, and permission, all rolled into one. He reached up and slid his hand to the back of her neck. In a second, he was where *he* wanted to be, with his mouth on hers and his fingers threading through her hair and her hands on his shoulders tugging him closer to her.

But another second later, she pulled back just as she had done when Scott had run into the living room.

"No." She pushed the afghan aside and rose from the couch, moved to perch on the arm of the chair, and crossed her arms. "I can't do this, Jason. I can't...go back there again."

"Who says we're going back anywhere? We're here now."

"And falling right back into the way we used to be. A way that's only going to create more problems. That's all it ever did."

"What about the good times? The fun times? The reason we got married in the first place? Don't try to tell me it was just because we liked making out and wanted to go the extra mile."

She said nothing.

He frowned. "You know it was always more than that. Don't you?" Her shrug hit him like a fist to the gut. *"Layne."*

"All right, yes, it was more than that. But outside of bed, we had a lot of problems. *I* had a lot of problems, only I didn't know it until now. I'm a failure with relationships, Jason. And I don't think I even know what love is."

"That's a load of bull." He went to her and took her hands. "Sweetheart, you are way too hard on yourself. I've been around here for a week now, and I see how you are with the kids. How much you care about them. If that's not love, I don't know what is. And if you could see yourself the way I do, you'd never call yourself a failure again. At anything."

"TIME TO GO, SCOTT," Jason said.

Holding Jill, Layne stood near the doorway in Rhea's playroom and watched as he rumpled her son's hair. When Scott slipped into his jacket, Jason waited, smiling down at him, already knowing Scott wanted to do up his buttons himself.

She cradled Jill against her and couldn't help but think of what Jason had said last night. Every time she recalled his words of support, his warm hands gently squeezing hers, the look in his eyes… Every time she thought of any of those, she melted a little more inside.

At the same time, she cautioned herself to keep from getting carried away. She *couldn't* fall for the boy who had dumped her and abandoned her son. Yet in spite of all the warnings, it was too late. She had done just that— given him her heart again.

But *was* he the same Jason who had once broken that heart?

Day by day, he grew closer to Scott and seemed even more comfortable around Jill. He had become more and more like the loving, caring father she had always thought he would be. Still, she couldn't set aside her biggest fear. Once he left, would he forget all about the kids the way he'd forgotten about her?

Scott waved goodbye to Rhea and took Jason's hand.

As they walked to the truck, Scott said, "Go home now, Jason. Go color."

"No, not today. I've got a surprise for you."

Layne stared at him, wondering what he had in mind. A trip to the store for more coloring books or a bigger box of crayons? Another toy for the baby?

"What, Jason? What?" Scott asked.

"You're having supper with Shay and Mo tonight."

Scott clapped his hands. "I love Grandma Mo and I love Shay. And I love the chickens."

She swallowed hard. Though she was burning up inside, her lips felt frozen. Somehow, she managed a smile for her son. Once in a while when Shay babysat the kids, rather than stay in their apartment, she would take them home to visit with her grandmother. Scott always enjoyed the trips to their small farm. But this wonderful surprise for her son only set off more warnings signals inside her.

Why would Jason feel he could take it upon himself to set up a visit?

Smiling, he held the passenger door for her. Then, without a word, he went around the truck to Scott, who was already standing by the driver's side, waiting for Jason to buckle him into his car seat.

When they pulled away from Miss Rhea's house, Layne glanced at Jason. He was focused on his driving and, judging by his slight smile, aware of her scrutiny and deliberately avoiding looking back at her. Keeping her in suspense as to what the rest of his surprise was about. She wondered what he had in mind for her—because it couldn't be a trip to the L-G Store.

"How did you arrange all this?" she asked as casually as she could.

"I talked to Shay while you were at work."

"And *why* did you arrange all this?"

"It's called 'Mama's Night Off.'"

"What does that mean?"

"It means you've got the night to yourself. No kids. No cooking. No cares."

She shook her head. "Well, you've got that partly right, anyhow. But you've forgotten about Jill. I'll need to nurse her before too long."

"Jill's going with Scott. But I've got that covered. Miss Rhea said the baby didn't take her extra bottle today. We can drop it off at Shay's along with the kids."

"You didn't arrange that, too?" she asked sharply.

He shot a glance at her. "Thanks. Do you really think I'd conspire to keep Jill from getting her milk?"

"I'm sorry." She flushed. She had been so focused on finding out what he was up to, she hadn't watched how she worded the question. "I just meant you might have asked Rhea to space out the bottle feedings a little more."

"Well, I didn't. And Jill doesn't always take her extra bottle."

His confident knowledge of her daughter's habits made her breath catch.

"Besides," he went on, "if there hadn't been a bottle left, I'd have adjusted my plans to let you get a feeding in."

"*Plans?* I knew it. You *do* have more in mind than just giving me a night off." Why did the thought both irritate and excite her?

"Oh, I've got *big* plans for you tonight, sweetheart. When we get home, I'm running you a nice warm bath and then letting you slip into something comfortable…"

"Jason."

"I was thinking of your fuzzy blue robe. And while you're unwinding, I'm heading over to SugarPie's to pick up supper for us and then to the Big Dipper to grab a pint of your favorite ice cream."

"Oh, really? And what's the point of all this? Because if you're thinking what I *think* you're thinking—" She stopped, too tongue-tied and tense—and maybe too turned-on—to keep track of where she was headed with all those thoughts.

She was as determined as ever to protect her kids. Yet she seemed to have lost her ability to protect herself. Despite everything, she wanted this night with Jason. She wanted playfulness and understanding and kisses and more.

He braked to a stop at the next intersection and turned to smile at her. "It's like I said yesterday, sweetheart. You're too tough on yourself. About everything. You need a break, and since I know you won't take one on your own, I'm stepping in to take charge."

Chapter Fifteen

"Who knew all you'd need to seduce a woman was a pint of chocolate-marshmallow swirl."

"*Ha.*" With the ice-cream spoon halfway to her mouth, Layne paused to roll her eyes at Jason, who sat at the opposite end of the couch. "You're not seducing me, you're helping me satisfy a craving."

"Great. Then maybe when you're done eating, you can help satisfy one of mine."

Again, she froze with the spoon halfway to her mouth. He had turned her innocent comment into a trigger for memories that left her breathless. She struggled for something to say, something to keep the moment light. "You're *pregnant*?" she managed finally. At the look of confusion on his face, she laughed. "Just kidding. I only meant, this is what I craved when I was carrying Jill."

"With dill pickles? Isn't that what all pregnant women are supposed to want? Pickles and ice cream?"

She shook her head. "Not me. The ice cream was good enough. Well…good anyway. But I just couldn't get enough of it." She tugged on the belt of her freshly washed robe, a silent reminder not to overdo it tonight.

He watched her movement but didn't comment on it. She felt too warm in the robe, but the last thing she could do was take it off in front of him. She was overly warm from her bath…or maybe from the way he sat looking at her, as if *he* couldn't get enough.

All during her bath, she had considered everything that had happened this week. She had tried to make herself believe she and Jason could work things out. She told herself he had arranged this Mama's Night Off—this *Date Night*?—especially for her. She kept reminding herself he was still here.

"What did you want when you were pregnant with Scott?" he asked.

"Potato chips and grape jelly." His eyes widened in horror. She laughed again—and then realized she couldn't remember the last time she had laughed this much in one night. "Don't knock the combination till you've tried it."

"No, thanks. But I wouldn't say no to a taste of that ice cream."

"I *knew* you wouldn't be satisfied with plain old vanilla." She waggled the carton, giving him permission to take a spoonful.

He moved closer. "I wasn't thinking of taking it from the container." His gaze drifted to her mouth.

Again, she froze. Not with a spoon in her hand this time, but from the thought running through her head. The thought of the kiss he so obviously wanted. The one she couldn't help wanting, too. It would be crazy to give in, and still… Nervously, she licked her lip. He seemed to take that as another sign of permission.

He leaned down, barely brushing her mouth with his, then paused, teasing her into a moan of pure frustration.

"Jason."

"Hmm?"

"I thought you wanted a taste."

"I did."

"Did?" She stared up at him.

He laughed. "Just wasn't sure how much *you* wanted a taste of plain old vanilla."

"Try me."

"That's the sweetest offer I've had all night."

He touched her mouth with his again. This time he lingered, and all her frustration went away. Yet his teasing never stopped. He kissed her once, a kiss sweeter than her offer, sweeter even than their ice cream. He kissed a trail from her mouth to her chin to her jawline. Then he brushed aside her robe to expose that one special spot he knew at the base of her throat.

Yes, he knew that spot. And so much more about her. They had shared so much—a marriage, a bed, a child.

She shivered, a small tremble sparked by a longing for what they had once had together and had let slip away.

He ran one hand down the lapel of her robe, slid the other along her bare thigh. This time, she shivered in anticipation. The glow of the lamp turned his light brown eyes into the soft, dark gold of melting caramel. It highlighted his face, showing her the grown-up version of the boy she had always loved.

"I've wanted to see you out of this thing from the minute I saw you *in* it." He tugged on the belt of her robe.

She stiffened. His hand stilled. With a little laugh, she shook her head. "Don't mind me." Blushing, she admitted, "That tug brought back memories. When I carried Jill, I craved ice cream constantly. Pulling my belt was my reminder not to go too crazy. A warning to stop."

He stared down at the belt. After a long moment, he tucked the front of her robe into place and smoothed the lapels again. Then he retreated to the opposite end of the couch.

She frowned. "Jason…? What…*exactly*…just happened here?"

"I got the memo."

She had lost all desire to laugh. Lost all desire for anything. Now she was the one confused. "*What* memo?"

"A warning to stop."

She flushed, too hot in her robe again. Too embarrassed by what she had anticipated, what she had waited for and wanted. Too hurt by his rejection. But she had to let him know he hadn't done anything wrong. "I didn't mean it as a warning for *you*."

"Didn't say you had. I sent the memo to myself. Look, Layne, I think—" He took a deep breath. "Maybe we need a break. It would be good for…for us both. There's a rodeo in Fort Worth this weekend. Not more than seven or eight hours from here. I can be there and home in a day."

He was running away. She could see it clearly in his face, could feel the distance widen between them although neither of them had moved. "You're backing off," she said flatly.

"Like I said, I'm just thinking about giving us a break. Until we sort things out. I'm paying attention to what you told me, that we're always good at getting wild and crazy but for nothing other than that."

"And now you finally decide to remember what I said? Right now, you conveniently decide to take it seriously?" She could hear her voice rising as if it were someone else's, something out of her control. She *felt* out of control, crushed by what he had done and stunned by memories flashing like fireworks in her mind. Worse, she felt betrayed by her own failure to remember this was Jason, who had walked out on her once before.

Why was she so upset? He had always run. To the rodeo. To the Cantina. To his friends.

Taking a deep breath, she tugged her robe more firmly closed around her. "On second thought, your timing's lousy but I think you've got the right idea. And when you get back—" *if you get back*... "—I also think it's time you found your room at the Hitching Post."

"You want me to leave?"

"Yes. This…whatever it was, was a big mistake. I've already told you I can't go back to what we had before. I'm not *who* I was before."

"So I suggest a break and you decide to kick me out. *Again*." He laughed bitterly. "I should have expected it. It sums up our entire relationship, doesn't it? Wild and crazy—or nothing. Your way or the highway."

She gasped. "*My* way?" She struggled to keep her voice low. To stay in control. "You're the one who left."

"Yeah, because you kicked me out then, too." He stood. "I'll go. But I want the right to see Scott. Not just for a week in the summer or a few days at Christmas. I want to set up regular visitations."

"Why? You won't be here. You'll leave Cowboy Creek and disappear again. You'll make promises you won't keep. Terry did that, too. And I won't let that happen to Scott again."

"I never broke any promises to him."

Now it was her turn to laugh bitterly. "Of course not. How could you? You'd never even met him."

HE DROVE THROUGH the night, making it halfway to Fort Worth before giving up. He turned back toward Cowboy Creek again, knowing the rodeo wasn't going to give him what he wanted. Not knowing where else to go.

The day started off on a dark note with the sun struggling to escape a bank of black clouds. A perfect match to his mood. By the time he pulled into the parking area behind the Hitching Post, the clouds had lifted but his mood stayed the same.

He found Jed sitting in a rocker on the back porch, watching the few horses standing in the corral, their manes ruffling in the breeze.

"Have a seat." Jed nodded toward the rocking chair beside his. "You look a mite out of sorts."

"Yeah. I've left Layne's," he admitted. His first inclination when he'd driven away from her apartment had been to head back to Dallas to stay. But what would that accomplish except to rob him of the chance to say goodbye to Scott?

He should have swung by Shay's farm to see the kids, but in the heat of the moment, the thought hadn't occurred to him.

In the middle of the night, he'd known he had to return to Cowboy Creek. Hours later, he had found himself turning the truck onto the long road to Garland Ranch, a place where he had always felt comfortable. And yet he perched on the seat of his rocker, feeling too edgy to sit back and relax.

"Leaving a place shouldn't make a man look this upset," Jed said. "Unless, of course, he didn't go on his own terms."

"We had a fight," he confessed. "A bad one."

Jed nodded and set his rocker into motion. "Well, it's not uncommon for people to scrap when they're trying to get used to living together—which is essentially what you two were doing this week."

"We'd already lived together." That hadn't worked out, either.

"Yeah, but you were still in the newlywed stage back then. You're different people now."

Just what Layne had said. *I'm not* who *I was before.* And he'd walked out on her. Again.

What had happened to the better man he'd become?

To his surprise, Jed chuckled. "When it came to arguments, my Mary and I had a few doozies after we were first hitched. To tell you the truth, much later on, we both admitted we had our doubts the marriage would last."

"I'm glad yours did. Mine didn't."

"You weren't alone, son. You and Layne each had a hand in whatever went wrong. The going was tough, I'll grant you that. You were both youngsters, both immature. But I can see you're a changed man, even if you can't tell the difference. You've got to put the past behind you and think about today."

The wooden rockers of Jed's chair against the porch let out a squeak. The sound made him think of the noise the weather vane on the barn back in Dallas made in a high wind. On long nights when he couldn't sleep, that weather vane kept him company. It soothed him, the way Jed obviously was attempting to do now.

Still, he had to confess. "Yeah, I've changed. But our conversation last night wasn't the best example of showing that."

"Then think about this week. Look how much you've done for Layne since you've been back."

She sure didn't see it that way. She had done nothing

but put up her guard. Resist. Fight back at almost every turn. And then kick him out.

"Speaking of doing things…" Jed began.

He stiffened on the edge of his seat. The older man stared out toward the corral as if he'd seen one of the mares take flight in the wind. Or as if he suddenly didn't want to make eye contact. Jason tightened his grip on his Stetson.

"That brings me to another point. We've got a room available now. And as you're not going to be doing much at Layne's, I've got a proposition for you." Jed looked over at him again. "One of the boys has asked for some time off. With Pete still on his honeymoon, that leaves us short on men around here. If you're willing to help out, we could use an extra hand."

Again, his first inclination was to rely on Dallas, to use that as his excuse to get away from Cowboy Creek—and away from the memory of his argument with Layne.

And again, he knew he couldn't just walk away. Not when he hadn't said goodbye to Scott or Jill or made arrangements with Layne to see his son. "I can stay on for a few days," he agreed, settling back into the rocker. Working here would give him a reason to hang around. It could give Layne some time to calm down.

And with luck, it would let him get past the fact he'd done all he could and she still didn't trust him.

JASON WOULD HAVE chosen the bunkhouse over staying at the hotel, but Jed had insisted he take the room promised to him. He had also invited him to eat supper with the Garlands.

"We're short two at the family table with Pete and

Jane away," he had said. "We'd be happy for the extra company."

To tell the truth, he had enjoyed the meal as well as the time with Jed's family. They had kept him from dwelling on thoughts of Layne and the kids. That could explain why, after supper, he got up from the table and made his way with everyone else to the Hitching Post's sitting room.

He took a seat in a leather high-backed chair that was comfortable but didn't seem made for him, the way Layne's stuffed armchair did. Maybe familiarity had made it feel that way. In just a few short days, he'd gotten used to staying in the apartment, taking walks with Layne and the kids, and even sleeping in that armchair.

"Jason?" Jed said in a loud voice. "You with us?"

So much for keeping his thoughts in check. "I'm here." He patted his stomach. "I'm about ready to nod off after all that good food, though. Paz, you're one heck of a cook."

She waved a hand. "It's nothing. But I thank you. And now I'll go back to the kitchen. You know where that is, Jason, if you need a snack later."

Paz had always wanted to feed him as if, like Mrs. B, she had somehow known he didn't get many home-cooked meals. "I doubt I'll get hungry again anytime soon after that meal, Paz. But I'll keep it in mind, especially if you're talking leftovers."

"That will be an option," Jed said. "She cooks enough for an army."

"You have a small platoon here, even without any hotel guests." Almost a dozen people were scattered around the room, more than half of them Jed's granddaughters and their kids, with a husband and a fiancé thrown in. "And that's not counting the newlyweds."

"Nothing like having family around," Jed said contentedly.

Again, Jason's thoughts strayed. This time, to Scott... His family.

On the other side of the room, Cole and Mitch were helping a couple of Jed's great-grandkids set up a plastic corral for a herd of toy horses. Jason wandered that way. "Need an extra pair of hands?"

Mitch looked up. "Always. In fact, you can take my place. I'm going to check on the baby. She's teething and on the cranky side."

"You put her teething rings in the refrigerator? That's what Layne does."

The other man laughed. "Looks like she's breaking you in right."

Or breaking me down.

He took a seat on the floor beside Cole and Tina's son, Robbie, who was a couple of years older than Scott.

"You can help," Robbie said, handing over two plastic pieces of the fence.

"What are we doing?"

"Making a corral for the horses. The other corral was just boxes. Just pretend. But this one's for real."

"Well, let me see what I can do."

"Speaking of real," Cole said, "I hope you've got some fence-repairing skills. We've got a stretch of pasture that needs some work done on it."

Judging by his lack of success with Layne, he didn't have any fence-mending skills at all. Still, he nodded. "I think I can handle that, boss." As acting manager while Pete was away, Cole would give him his orders.

He didn't see why they couldn't work together—as long as the subject of Layne didn't come up.

"Jason, how's Layne feeling?" Cole's wife, Tina, asked.

So much for that thought of his, too. "Fine. I think she's just about over her flu."

"Well, that's good to hear," Jed said. "She's got to make it out this way for dinner this weekend ."

"I'm sure she's looking forward to that." He glanced at Robbie. "Scott's been talking about you and your horses. I know he wants to come for the visit, too."

"He likes horses."

"And cars and coloring." He couldn't help but smile as he recalled Scott's crayon stubs and his excitement over getting a new coloring book.

As he reached for another section of fencing, he caught Cole's gaze on him. He expected a stony-eyed stare but was surprised to see the other man's thoughtful expression. He recalled what Cole had said to him about Layne.

I'll break your neck before I let you break her heart again.

Cole appeared mellow enough now, but things weren't always the way they seemed. Instead, the man could easily be plotting ways to make good on his threat.

Chapter Sixteen

Jason reined in and dismounted, then handed the reins of his mount over to the stable boy. A few yards away, Cole did the same.

They had spent some long, chilly hours out on the ranch during these past couple of days fixing the fence line, checking on the water pipe Cole had repaired and moving some of the herd to a pasture with more vegetation. Casual conversation wasn't much on their agenda, but the talking they had done had been civil.

Inside the barn, they found Jed and Robbie in front of Daffodil's stall.

"Hi, Daddy. Hi, Jason." Robbie stood on a small stool feeding Daffodil a carrot. "Daffy's hungry."

"She's not the only one." Jed laughed. He turned to explain to Jason. "When Paz gives Robbie a carrot for Daffodil, she gives him a cookie for himself."

Jason laughed, too. "I'll bet Daffodil is the best-fed horse in the stable."

"You wouldn't be far wrong," Cole said from the workbench near the office. "Robbie's got quite a sweet tooth."

"Yeah, Scott, too. Especially when it comes to syrup on his pancakes."

"I like chocolate candy," Robbie announced. "And chocolate chips in my pancakes."

"So does Scott. That's his second favorite after the syrup."

Jed clapped Robbie on the shoulder. "Well, Daffodil's about finished, and we need to get back to the house and clean up for supper."

"That makes two of us," Jason said.

"You coming, Cole?" Jed asked.

"No, you all go ahead. I've got some work to catch up on. I'll be there in a bit."

When the three of them left the barn, Robbie ran ahead to the Hitching Post's back porch. Jason walked beside Jed, who seemed content to amble.

Unlike Cole, the older man always had talk on his agenda. "Looks like you've gotten to know a lot about Scott's preferences in just the week or so you've been here."

"And gotten to miss him in just these couple of days."

"They'll all be here for a few hours tomorrow."

"Yeah." A few hours, and what then? Layne would go back home and do her best to keep herself and the kids away from him. In the short time before he had to leave town again, his chances of getting her to agree to visitations with Scott would be slim.

His chances of her ever trusting him were already nonexistent.

In their last conversation, her words and tone of voice and expression had all told him more than she probably wanted him to know. Jill's daddy had hurt Layne badly. The way he'd let down both kids had hurt her even more. The experience had left her without any faith in men altogether, and especially in the two she'd once married.

She would always compare her first husband to her second one, and in her eyes, they would both always come out looking the same.

He couldn't worry any more about getting Layne to trust him. She might never let down her guard, and he would have to live with what he had done to make her raise it. But he couldn't live any longer without seeing his son on a regular basis. No matter how reluctant she was to grant them, he would fight for his rights.

Beside him, his companion had gone silent as if he were somehow aware of the thoughts filling his mind. Jason adjusted the brim of his Stetson, cleared his throat, and sighed.

"You might as well come out with it, boy," Jed said quietly. "You're about as easy to read as one of Robbie's schoolbooks."

He pictured Scott with his storybooks and recalled how raptly his son paid attention while his daddy turned the pages and read to him. He thought about when he might next have a chance to spend time with Scott. Reality hit, and his heart thudded.

The reaction told him even frequent visitations wouldn't be enough.

He needed to be able to drop by on the spur of the moment to take Scott to the park or for ice cream, to bring him a new coloring book, to read him another story, to tuck him into bed. He couldn't pass up any chance to be with his son. Which meant he couldn't leave Cowboy Creek.

"Jed, you said you were shorthanded with Pete gone, and I know he and Jane are coming back home tonight. But some of the hands were telling me you'd mentioned needing another man around the place. I'd like to head back to Dallas and work out my notice, then pick up the rest of my gear and get back here as soon as I can. I'd like to fill the job permanently, if you'll have me."

"I'm more than willing to take you on. You ought to know that." Jed clapped him on the shoulder the way he'd done to Robbie. "I'm just thankful you've decided to come to your senses."

By Saturday, Layne felt well enough to take on a few more hours at SugarPie's.

When they reached a brief lull just before the noon rush, Sugar took her aside in one corner of the shop's kitchen. "I don't want you wearing yourself out."

"I'll be fine. I'm feeling much better, and I've been catching up on sleep." To tell the truth, since Jason had left, she had gone to bed early both nights to keep from sitting alone in the living room. If she felt his absence so strongly after this short time, she didn't want to imagine how Scott must feel.

She set an empty teapot beneath the hot water spout and watched to make sure she filled the pot to the brim. "Mrs. Browley just came in, and you know how she likes her tea." She liked to tip well, too, and Layne could use all the tips she could get. With the refrigerator and pantry emptying, she was back to needing extra money to make up for the days she had been sick. She couldn't— and wouldn't—count on Jason's offer of help.

In the small back office off the kitchen, the telephone rang. "I'll get that," Sugar said.

"I'll take this out." Carrying a tray with the teapot on it, she left Sugar and went into the dining area of the shop.

"Well, this is lovely," Mrs. Browley said. "Why don't you sit and have a cup with me, Layne?"

A quick look around the shop showed no new customers had come in. Sugar had stayed in the kitchen and must still be on the phone or she would certainly have joined them by now. "I'll pass on the tea, thanks. But I can sit and chat for a minute." She perched on the edge of the bench seat.

"I was disappointed not to have you and Jason and the children stop in to see me again."

"I've been on the run quite a bit." On the run from thoughts of Jason. "And I'm working extra hours today. Scott's still talking about your cookies, though. He loved them."

"Well, there will be more waiting for you when you stop in. I made another batch of chocolate chip today. They're Jason's favorites, too, you know. He used to eat them by the dozen when he was a boy."

"You baked cookies for him?"

"I did. And I cooked for him, too, when I could get him to sit down long enough to eat. His mother wasn't good at much but making frozen dinners and ordering takeout. He was too proud to stop by often—though I could always entice him with the chocolate chips."

Just as he had enticed her with a pint of chocolate-marshmallow swirl ice cream. She didn't want to think about his treat or the taste of vanilla ice cream on his lips. She didn't want to recall her Mama's Night Off or—most especially—the way that night had ended.

"Are you having your Saturday usual, Mrs. Browley?" The "usual" was pastrami on rye with extra mustard and two dill pickles. Even before she had filled the teapot, she could have had Sugar make the sandwich. After Mrs.

Browley had nodded, Layne smiled and stood. "Be back in a few minutes."

In the kitchen, she relayed the order.

"As I figured." Sugar had already set out the rye bread. But she frowned. "Are you sure you're all right to work?"

"I'm fine, really. And I'll have some time tomorrow to take it easy."

And the rest of the day forced to be around Jason.

"You still planning on going out to Jed's?" Sugar asked.

She nodded. Normally, she looked forward to their visits to Garland Ranch, but not this one. How could she miss Jason so much at the apartment and yet dread the idea of seeing him at the Hitching Post? She almost winced at the echo of what he had said at the Big Dipper when she didn't want to let him go off with Scott and had refused to leave Jill alone with him.

At your apartment, you were willing enough to take my help. But now we're out in public, something's different?

She had denied it, of course, and would deny it now. But somewhere inside, she knew the truth. The fewer people who saw her relying on him, the easier it would be for her to save face once he'd left.

"Oh, yes," she told Sugar, "we're still going out to the ranch. Scott's ecstatic about getting to play with Robbie and his horses and maybe go for a ride on Bingo." Yet this morning, he had seemed uninterested when she mentioned their visit, and the motorway Jason had made for him lay pushed aside in the corner of the living room.

She hoped he wasn't coming down with the flu. But

she suspected his listlessness came from the same reasons that had made her go to bed early.

According to all reports—from Cole, from Tina, from Shay, and even from Sugar when she had arrived at work this morning—Jason was still at the Hitching Post. Almost everyone in town seemed to know where he had gone.

Everyone but Scott.

His puzzled expression reminded her so much of the man he still didn't know was his daddy. His questions nearly broke her heart.

Where Jason go, Mommy?
Jason read story tonight?
Jason come home tomorrow?

No, Jason wouldn't "come home tomorrow." But Scott would see him then. After dinner, they would leave the ranch, and all the questions would begin again.

Again, she weighed the difference between hit-or-miss visits and a real relationship and knew where Jason would fall in the balance.

"That was Jed on the phone," Sugar said casually.

"What's up? Did he say anything about tomorrow?" She grabbed the tongs and took a couple of pickles from the container in the refrigerated case.

"Just that he was looking forward to having you and the kids come for dinner."

"That's great."

"Oh, and that Jason's heading back to Dallas."

The cold container slipped from her fingers and hit the preparation counter, spewing pickle juice over the clean surface. She lunged for the paper towel dispenser and wiped the spill before the juice could drip to the floor. Gaze focused on her task, she said, "Jason's leaving?" Even to her own ears, her voice sounded high and tight and thready.

"Yes. Jed said he's eager to get back home."

"I can imagine. He's been here for a while now."

A while she couldn't hope would last forever.

He had never said a word about seeing her again, and she could live with that. But what had happened to his claim he wanted a relationship with Scott? To his plan to talk to her about rights and visitation?

"I'll take this sandwich out," Sugar said. "Layne, you ought to sit down. You're looking very pale all of a sudden."

She waited till Sugar had left, then sank onto the high wooden stool beside the counter. Turning pale was the least of her reactions.

She had been tearing herself up inside about the way her last conversation with Jason had ended. Now, she gave thanks she hadn't made any agreements with him. She gave more thanks she hadn't told him she'd given him her heart again. All those yearnings to relent and trust him, all those wants and hopes and dreams, had come to nothing—just as their wild and crazy relationship had always been destined to arrive at that same end.

She wasn't wrong about him. He was walking away from her and, worse, walking away from her son.

If he could leave without even saying goodbye to Scott, why would he make any promises to come back?

Even if he *did* make promises, what did it matter, when she knew he would only break them?

Chapter Seventeen

After the hotel's breakfast buffet on Sunday, Jason wandered out to the corral. Robbie had asked to go for a ride on Bingo, the small Shetland Jed kept for the kids. Cole was standing outside the corral fence, watching his son as the stable hand led him and the pony into the corral.

Robbie mounted without help, then took up the reins. Bingo started off at a leisurely trot.

Cole looked about ready to burst with pride.

Jason could understand the feeling. "Looks like a pro already."

Cole nodded. "He's got a ways to go, but he's getting there. He's had some experience."

"Good thing. A kid living on a ranch needs to feel at home in the saddle."

For a few minutes, they watched Robbie and Bingo.

Eventually, Cole said, "Scott comes out to ride once in a while. He's not as comfortable on horseback, but then, Layne never has the time to run him out here for some practice."

Wondering if that was a dig at him for not being around to lighten Layne's workload, he looked at the other man.

I'll teach him to ride, he wanted to say. *I'll be around from now on*.

But he hadn't told anyone except Jed about his plans.

"Being a mama's not easy," he said instead.

"Or a daddy. Either way, it's a challenge, let me tell you. But one I wouldn't give up. Some folks aren't cut out for the responsibility, though."

Here it comes. The blast he'd been expecting since he'd first seen the man again. He tightened his grip on the fence rail, intending to keep the same tight hold on his temper.

"Terry was worthless," Cole continued, surprising him. "Scott missed out on a lot of things while he was in the picture. Still, kids catch on fast, given the right start. A couple of years putting in some riding time, and he'll be Robbie's age and looking like a pro, too."

"Yeah." He had to swallow hard past the lump in his throat. *I'd like to be around for those years. I've missed too many other important ones*.

He missed his son. For about the thousandth time that morning, he shot another look at his watch to make sure the second hand was still moving. According to Jed's estimate, Scott and Jill and Layne should be arriving soon.

"Kids catch on," Cole said again, "but we can't catch up. And it's not easy knowing we can't turn back time."

"What good would that do? Things would all just turn out the same."

"I imagine some would and some wouldn't. But the truth is, nobody knows which. There's no point in worrying over it. Like I told Layne, all we can do is go forward."

"I'm trying that for Scott's sake, but your sister doesn't seem inclined to go along."

"That could be. Remember when you and Layne first came to me about you two getting married?"

He nodded.

"I talked to her afterward. I was dead set against sign-ing the paperwork and wanted her to give it some time, to wait until she was of age. But she kept coming at me with reasons until she hit on the one that made me say yes." Cole stared at him for a moment, his gaze level and his expression neutral. "You need to find another way to state your case."

After a moment, Cole leaned on the rail and went back to watching the activity in the corral.

He did the same, both surprised and pleased at the man's show of support. They stood there in silence. As he watched Cole's little boy on the Shetland, he pictured his son's face and he heard his son's laugh.

It took him a minute to realize the laughter wasn't just in his mind.

Cole turned back toward the Hitching Post before he did.

"Uncle Cole!" Scott called, sounding more excited than Jason had ever heard him before.

He turned.

Scott spotted him. *"Jason!"* he shrieked, more excited still. He ran across the yard toward them, not headed for his uncle, not focused on Robbie or Bingo, but running right to *him* with his arms outstretched.

Dropping into a crouch, he caught his son in a bear hug. His throat tightened. He tried to speak but couldn't get out a word. Instead, he buried his face against his boy's baby-soft hair. And he wished with everything in him that he had the power to turn back time.

LAYNE WATCHED JASON hug Scott and suddenly felt as light-headed as if she'd been hit with another round of the flu.

They were both oblivious to her approach, but Cole stood watching her. By the time she reached them, Jason had settled her son on his hip. Scott rested his head against Jason's chest. Starbursts of pain exploded in her head. She put one hand on the corral railing to steady herself.

"Cole," she said quietly, "could you take Scott in to see Grandpa Jed?"

"Sure."

He reached for Scott, who clung to Jason. "Wanna stay, Mommy. *Please?*"

"You...you can see Jason again in a little while, honey. But I know Grandpa Jed and Paz want to see you, too."

"C'mon, Scotty."

Cole reached for him, and this time, Scott went without protest. He waved at them over Cole's shoulder. "Bye, Jason. Bye, Mommy."

They both said goodbye and waved in return.

As soon as Cole and Scott were out of earshot, she turned to Jason. "What are you doing? Isn't it bad enough you're leaving? Do you have to make sure Scott's even more attached to you before you go?"

"Who says I'm leaving?"

"Sugar says. And Jed told her, so please don't try to tell me it's not true."

"I'm not leaving Scott again, no matter what."

"Right. As if I can't see through that. I've fielded enough lies and broken promises when it comes to my son."

"*Our son*, dammit." He slammed his hand on the

fence rail. "The least you can do is acknowledge I'm his daddy. And you're jumping to conclusions without giving me a chance, the way you did years ago when you threw me out. I've done everything I can think of to make amends, to show you I'm sorry for walking away." He swallowed visibly and took a deep breath. "Get this. I…am…not…leaving. Not this time. Not permanently. Jed's hired me on, and I'm headed back to Dallas only to pick up all my gear."

He took another, deeper breath and let it out more slowly. "I didn't lie about wanting a relationship with Scott—an ongoing relationship. I want to be here to see him whenever I can. If there's nothing else we can agree on, I hope we can come to terms on that."

Her vision blurred. "I can't trust you—"

"You *won't* trust me. That's what you mean. Layne, Terry doesn't want to see Jill. Or Scott. I want to see them both. I'm not Terry. But you're never going to see me for who I am, are you?" Again, he took a breath. "You've made me a victim in the fallout from your second divorce. All right, I can deal with that, one way or another. But by cutting me off from Scott, you've made him a victim, too. And that's something I can't handle."

"You sure you won't stay to supper and just head out in the morning?" Jed frowned. For some reason, Jason had made a last-minute change of plans. "We're having a celebration, after all, with the newlyweds home again. And anyhow, I thought you were staying the rest of the weekend."

The boy wouldn't meet his eyes, just stood shaking his head. "The sooner I get to Dallas, the sooner I can be back."

"And you *will* be back?" That earned him a look.

"Of course."

"Does this sudden rush to leave town have something to do with Layne?"

Jason sighed. "Jed, *everything* has to do with Layne, one way or another. She's Scott's mama. But to answer you directly, no. No matter what she says or thinks, I'm coming back to stay."

"Well, that's good to hear. Your room'll be waiting."

Jason shook his head. "I'm not going to tie up one of your hotel rooms. When I get back, I'll bunk down with the rest of the hands."

"What for? You're family." This time, his comment brought a laugh.

"I'm the ex-husband of your grandson-in-law's sister."

"That's good enough for me."

"Thanks. But I'll still take the bunkhouse." Jason reached out to shake hands. "I'll call you once I talk to my ranch manager and know the date I'll be headed back."

"You do that." Leaning against the porch rail, he watched while the boy went around to the parking area and climbed into his pickup truck. He continued to watch until the truck became a mere speck in the road.

He was standing in the same position a few minutes later when Tina and Paz came out onto the porch.

"We've been looking all over for you," Tina said. "It's almost time to eat. What are you doing out here?"

"Seeing Jason off."

"Off?" Paz repeated. She sank onto the porch swing and looked at him in dismay.

"Where is he going?" Tina asked.

"Back to Dallas to pick up whatever he owns and come home."

"Home?" Paz echoed. "You mean home to Layne?"

"Or just home to Cowboy Creek?"

He shook his head at Tina. "Don't be so negative. The boy wanted a job here, and I've given it to him. That's one step he's taking in the right direction. I told him we'd have a room waiting—though he's insisting on bunking with the other hands. What I didn't bother mentioning was, I also have high hopes of keeping my successful matchmaking run going."

"Oh, I don't know, Abuclo. From the way he's been avoiding Layne this afternoon, it looks like he's given up on a reconciliation with her. And she might be even harder to convince."

"Don't be so sure. Yesterday, I specifically told Sugar to let Layne know Jason was leaving…but *not* that he planned to come back. The girl's reaction was everything we could have hoped for."

Paz gasped. "She was upset."

"Darned straight, she was. And that was my entire point—to show her just how she would feel if he took off again. She's still resisting, but I've got thoughts on how to handle that." He smiled. "Don't you worry, ladies, I'm not giving up. Those two are meant to be together. You know it. I know it. Now, we just have to help them see it, too."

FOR THE FIRST time in days, Layne heard boot steps in the hallway. At the triple tap on the door, she shook her head. Cole. Since her trip with the kids out to the Hitching Post on Sunday, he or Tina had called her daily. And now here he was in person.

When she opened the door, Scott greeted Cole with his usual enthusiasm, a shade less energetic than the way he had thrown himself into Jason's arms outside the corral. She blinked. Every replay she made of that moment left her misty-eyed.

"Checking up on me?" she asked, her voice unsteady.

"Just checking in. I had to stop by the hardware store again and figured I'd swing by."

"Good to see you." She led him into the kitchen. "What'll it be?"

He took a seat at the table, and if he noticed the absence of the extra place mat, he didn't comment on it. "Sweet tea. And maybe some sympathy."

"Sympathy?" she asked, startled, thinking immediately of Tina and the baby on the way. "What's wrong?"

"Nothing with me. I'm offering it to you."

She smiled wryly as she went to the refrigerator. "What makes you think I need it?"

"Sugar says you seem down."

"Just a delayed reaction from the flu."

"Is it? Or is it the result of what happened out at the ranch the other day?"

"You mean Scott's big hello to Jason?"

"No, I mean your reaction to Scott's big hello to Jason and then the fact he left town less than an hour after your conversation."

"Coincidence."

"I don't think so."

Though she tried to shrug off his statement, she couldn't fool Cole. As she set his glass of tea on the table, he gave her the big-brother look that had always made her fess up. And truthfully, she felt the need of a confession.

She took her seat across from him. "He said I'm making him a victim by comparing him too much to Terry. And he said…" she swallowed hard "…he said I'm making Scott a victim, too."

"And what did you say to that?" he asked, his tone so filled with concern he broke through her defenses without even trying.

Her laugh sounded more like a sob. "I didn't get to say anything. He just walked away, like he always does."

"All right, then what did you think about that?"

"I think *we* were victims. You and I. And I'm working at getting over that. But—" Her voice broke. "But I would never take anything out on Scott."

"Of course you wouldn't." He leaned forward. "I think Jason realizes that, too. You know how things get said in the heat of the moment. But you also saw how he was with Scott. He's attached to the boy whether you want him to be or not."

When she said nothing, he reached for her hand. "Layne, I've heard Jason talk about him, and he knows all the things a daddy ought to know about his son. What's more, I've heard the pride in his voice whenever he mentions Scott's name. I think the man regrets what happened, about not being around." Holding her gaze, he said gently, "And I think he deserves a second chance."

Chapter Eighteen

Jason parked the pickup truck outside Greg's house and rang the front doorbell. When he had called earlier, Greg had insisted he stop by.

Within seconds, his buddy stood in the open doorway grinning at him. "Well, come on in. I was beginning to think you were never going to make it back this way again. Beer?"

He nodded.

"And I've got a pizza in the oven. It's just us. My girls are out for the night."

The statement made him think of Mama's Night Off—and what a bad idea that had been.

He followed Greg into the kitchen and took a seat at the breakfast bar. When Greg handed him a longneck, they clinked their bottles together in a toast—although why they did that, he had no idea. "We celebrating something?"

"Considering on the phone you sounded as though you'd won a world final and your 'quick trip' to New Mexico lasted more than a week, I'd say your visit was a success. It wouldn't surprise me a bit if you'd found a reason to hang up your spurs, too. And that's cause for celebration in my book." Greg leaned on the counter. "You got to see your boy."

He nodded.

"So, who does he take after?"

"My ex in coloring, but he favors me in a few ways, too." He talked about their similarities and resemblances, then ran down a mental list of what he'd learned about his son in such a short time. Scott's liking for syrup, storybooks and wearing crayons down to nubs. "His favorite cookie is chocolate chip, just like mine."

"Hate to tell you, buddy, but *every* kid's favorite is chocolate chip."

"Now *that's* bull."

Greg laughed. He took the pizza pan out of the oven and proceeded to serve their supper—cutting one long line down the middle of the pizza, dividing it into halves. "Obviously, you saw your ex."

"Yeah."

"And?"

"And nothing."

"Then you're home again and that's it?"

"No. I'm giving notice and going back. I've got a job in Cowboy Creek."

Greg gave a long whistle. "That's more than *nothing*. Sounds like there must be some interest there."

"I'm not going back to *Layne*," he snapped.

"And sounds like I hit a sore spot."

"You talk too much. Anybody ever tell you that?"

"My wife. Constantly." Greg took a huge bite from his slice and sat chewing it as if to prove he could keep quiet if he wanted to.

"All right. It *is* a sore spot," he admitted. "If she had her way, I wouldn't get near my son."

Greg swallowed and shook his head. "That's bad. You need to do whatever it takes to get her to come around."

You need to find another way to state your case.

He needed to apologize.

On the long ride back here from Cowboy Creek, he'd run all his conversations with Jed and Cole and Layne through his head. He'd replayed all the times he had spent with Scott.

And now, hearing his best buddy stating essentially what Layne's brother had said, he'd finally come to his senses. Finally figured out the truth.

He and Layne both might have been to blame for what had happened before, but in the long run, this time around the fault was his. He'd wanted Layne to trust him. To forgive him.

Instead, he'd given her every reason to believe he would run.

When the knock came at the door, Layne's heart jumped to her throat.

The sound of Scott's happy squeal brought tears to her eyes.

Blinking them away, she opened the door. Jason stood in the hallway, and she didn't know where to look first. He looked good, so good, just as he had the day she'd first seen him standing there a couple of weeks ago.

She swept her gaze from his tousled hair to his caramel eyes to his dark-shadowed jaw. Finally, she looked down at her son, who had wrapped his arms around Jason's leg as if he never meant to let him go.

"You're back," she said.

"You noticed." He ruffled Scott's hair. He cleared his throat and shifted his Stetson from one hand to the other.

"I'm on my way out to the Hitching Post. Jed asked me to stop by. He's invited you and the kids for supper tonight. He said Tina tried to reach you but didn't get an answer."

"Really?" She frowned. "We've been here all afternoon. She must have called earlier when I was working. I wonder why she didn't leave a message, as usual."

"Beats me." He glanced down. "What do you say, Scott, want to go have supper with Grandpa Jed?"

Scott squealed again. "Yes-s-s. *Es-s-s.* Scott have supper. Jason have supper, too?"

"I sure will." He grinned at her son, then shot a look in her direction.

"Mommy have supper sure, too?" Scott asked.

After a hesitation, she said, "Yes, I sure will have supper, too." She had already promised Cole she and the kids would come back out to the ranch soon. She just hadn't expected Jason to be joining them, too.

She hadn't really believed he would come back.

"We've got a while before we have to be at the Hitching Post," he said.

"Oh." She looked at her son. "Scott, can you go put your cars away in your bedroom for Mommy?"

He nodded, stepping backward, his gaze still on Jason.

When he had gone to pick up his toys, she turned back to Jason and shrugged. "Can I get you anything?"

"A comfortable armchair and a few minutes of your time."

She hesitated, still hovering near the door. She could—*should*—tell him to leave. She and the kids could get out to the Hitching Post on their own. But curiosity and another feeling she didn't want to label won out.

She curled up on her corner of the couch. He took the

armchair. Seeing him sitting there made her heart do a little flip, half from pleasure, the other half from nerves. "Before you start, I owe you an apology."

He raised his brows in question.

"You were right about my not seeing you as you are. But it had nothing to do with Terry. Even when you and I first got married, I couldn't…didn't trust you completely."

"Because we fought so much."

"Yes." She took a deep breath and let it out again. "But that wasn't your fault, it was mine. Fighting and making up with you was my way of keeping you at a distance. Of not getting too close, so you wouldn't see I was someone you couldn't love."

"Why would you think that? I *always* loved you."

"I know that now. I wanted to believe it back then. And I did love you, Jason. I still do." Her voice broke. "But down deep, I didn't think you could love me. I didn't think anyone could." She linked her trembling fingers in her lap and stared at them.

As much as she had confided to him in the past, there were things she hadn't said. Things he deserved to know. "When I was growing up, my mother virtually ignored me, and my dad spent most of his time telling me how worthless I was. How no one would ever care about me. He did the same and worse to Cole, especially whenever Cole stepped in to help me."

A tear slipped down her cheek. She brushed it away. "I hated knowing that protecting me made things harder for him. But I don't know what I would have done without him. And then I met you. And *loved* you, right from the beginning. But after all those years of listening to my dad, I couldn't believe you would ever really care about me."

Jason moved to sit beside her and take her hand. "I didn't make things any better by fighting with you."

"What else could you do? You had to protect yourself." Stunned, she raised her hand to her mouth as if that would help her take back the words. "*You had to protect yourself*, the way Cole protected me. That makes me just like my father."

"No, it doesn't. It's not the same thing at all. And I was as bad as you were about the fighting. Only sometimes..." his smile made her hot all over "...it was all about the makeup sex." Then he shook his head. "Jed said to me we were young and immature. He was right. That's all it was. I saw pictures you kept of us from when we got married, and the one Sugar took of us the day we found out you were pregnant. We were having a baby, Layne, and we were still kids ourselves."

He swallowed so hard, she could see the muscles in his neck strain. "We were probably scared without even realizing it," he continued. "And we sure had to be stressed. That's partly why I started following the rodeo."

She stiffened.

"Hear me out." He wrapped his arm around her as if afraid she would get up and walk away. "Yeah, I like riding, but it was more than that. I was worried to hell and back—about being a daddy, about taking care of you and the baby, about paying the bills and providing everything you'd need. It was the thought of winning one of those big purses that drove me to the circuit. And the more you argued with me about it, the more stressed I got."

Again, he shook his head. "It's no wonder we fought so much. Or that you kicked me out. That last night—"

"I don't want to talk about it."

"We have to." He brushed his chin against her hair. "That night, you didn't know where I went, and when I came back, you wouldn't let me explain. I know you figured I ran off to the Cantina and had myself a good time. But I didn't. I went home."

"Home?"

"Well," he amended, "to my mother's house. That's where I was headed anyway." He laughed softly. "Instead, I somehow wound up next door at the Browleys'. Mrs. B fed me supper and chocolate chip cookies." Suddenly, he sobered. "Later, when I tried to come home and you refused to let me anywhere near you, I decided it was time to go."

"I'm sorry," she whispered.

"I'm sorry, too. But I swear to you, I thought I was doing the right thing. I figured you were better off without me. I knew Cole would take care of you. I knew you had plenty of friends. It seemed the smart thing was just to make a clean break and a fresh start." He reached up to run his finger down her cheek, wiping away tears. "I'm sorry, Layne. I shouldn't have left."

"I didn't give you much choice." She rested her head against his chest. She could feel his heartbeat thumping, hear his indrawn breath.

He wrapped his arms around her and held her close. "Then I came back, and things weren't any better." His voice rumbled in her ear. "I wanted to see Scott, and I didn't plan to fight with you, but I guess you weren't the only one with deep-down troubles. I wanted you to forgive me for walking away, but I didn't see how you could. Because I couldn't forgive myself." He sighed. "I should have tried harder to keep us together."

"And I should have told you everything instead of pushing you away."

He leaned back and looked down at her. "I love you. Can we start over again?"

"No."

He sucked in a breath.

"Last week, I thought about that, too," she admitted. "But we can't start over. We already have Scott."

"And Jill."

"And Jill," she echoed, her heart swelling and her eyes filling with fresh tears. What a good man he was. What a good man he had been all along. "Jason... I need to tell you something else. The other day, Scott went into your wallet and pulled everything out of it. When I went to put things back, I found his birth announcement."

"And here I thought you'd just gone snooping."

"I wouldn't do that," she said, shocked. Then she caught his smile. "I know you saw Scott has my name. Jill does, too. I kept my maiden name when I married Terry because I knew..." She took a deep breath. "I knew I couldn't give any child we might have his name when I hadn't given Scott yours."

Now he took a deep breath. Tears turned his caramel-brown eyes to liquid gold. "Layne," he said hoarsely. He swallowed hard and ran his finger down her cheek. "Layne, will you marry me again?"

"Do you think we've learned enough to keep from making the same mistakes twice?"

"Yeah, I think we have."

"Then, no kicking anybody out. No walking away, ever again." She held his gaze. He didn't flinch. "And no more taking charge. We're equal partners now. Will you promise me?"

"Promise. Trust me?"

"Always." She touched his cheek.

He leaned down and kissed her, so long and so thoroughly, she barely registered the sound of Jill's cries from the bedroom and only belatedly felt Scott tugging on her sweater.

"Mommy, Jill crying."

"Yes," she said breathlessly. "I hear her."

Jason scooped up Scott and set him on his hip. Then he rose, pulling her to her feet along with him. "Let's go. We can't keep our hungry little girl waiting." He put his arm around her and escorted her down the hall and into the kids' bedroom.

She took a seat on the bed and watched as Jason expertly lifted the baby from her crib. Scott lay on the bed on one side of her, Jason stretched out on the other, and Jill settled down to nurse.

Across the room, she caught their reflection in the dresser mirror. And she smiled at the picture of the family they were meant to be.

Epilogue

Three weeks later

The clinking of utensils against champagne glasses made Jason grin. With one finger, he lifted his unresisting bride's chin to steal yet another kiss.

Once the noise died down, they broke apart, but he made sure to keep his arm wrapped around her.

Jed walked up and clapped Jason on the shoulder. "Well, thanks to you two, the Hitching Post has just set a new record for pulling together a wedding and reception with all the works."

Layne smiled. "I think you deserve some of the credit."

"And I guess I'll take it." Jed grinned. "I've got to confess, I do feel I had a hand in getting you together."

"That's for sure." He gave his bride a squeeze. "Now, how about we try for a record on baby showers?"

"I'm all for that," Jed agreed.

"Uhh…gentlemen?" Layne said. "If I have a vote in this decision, I say we wait just a bit. Besides, Tina's shower has to come first."

Jason nodded. "Fine. Whenever you're ready, I'll be here."

"I know you will." She rested her head on his shoulder. Then she said with a laugh, "As it is, since we got married so quickly, people probably think we already have a baby on the way."

"I can tell you exactly what folks in this town think," Jed announced.

"That doesn't surprise me," he murmured. Layne elbowed him in the ribs. Jed gave him a sharp-eyed glance.

Then the older man laughed. "Well, it's true I do like to know what goes on around here." He sobered and rested a hand on Layne's shoulder, too. "Folks think you two have grown up and *caught up* to where you were always meant to go. They couldn't be prouder of you two, and neither can I."

As he walked away, smiling, Jason held Layne closer. She looked up at him, her blue eyes shining with happy tears.

Robbie ran across the dance floor toward them, with Scott hard on his heels.

"My daddy says come and take a picture," Robbie announced.

"Daddy come, too?" Scott asked, taking Jason's hand.

Unable to answer, he simply nodded.

Three weeks had gone by since they had told Scott the news, and every time he heard his son call him Daddy, he still got a lump in his throat. Three weeks had passed since Layne had agreed to marry him—again—and he still couldn't believe his good fortune.

He gathered his new family around him for the photograph. Over their heads, he met Jed's gaze. And he sent a silent, heartfelt thank-you to the matchmaking grandpa who had helped to make his life complete.

* * * * *

*Jed Garland isn't finished with
his matchmaking ways!
Be sure to look for the next book in
Barbara White Daille's*
THE HITCHING POST HOTEL *series in 2017,
wherever Harlequin books and ebooks are sold!*

COMING NEXT MONTH FROM

H HARLEQUIN®
™

✎Western ❦Romance

Available August 2, 2016

#1605 A BULL RIDER'S PRIDE
Welcome to Ramblewood • by Amanda Renee
After a stay in the hospital, bull rider Brady Sawyer can't
get back into the arena fast enough. Which is against the
advice of Sheila Lindstrom, the doctor who put Brady back
together...and could possibly break his heart!

#1606 TEXAS REBELS: PHOENIX
Texas Rebels • by Linda Warren
Everything is changing for Phoenix Rebel. Not only has the
formerly carefree cowboy discovered he's the father to a
baby boy, he's also fallen in love with Rosemary McCray—a
sworn enemy of his family.

#1607 COURTED BY THE COWBOY
The Boones of Texas • by Sasha Summers
Kylee James keeps people at arm's length for good reasons.
Especially Fisher Boone. With her past dogging her, Kylee
knows the handsome cowboy deserves happiness, which is
something she could never give him...

#1608 THE KENTUCKY COWBOY'S BABY
Angel Crossing, Arizona • by Heidi Hormel
Former bull rider AJ McCreary has inherited a ranch in
Arizona and the timing is perfect—he needs to get off the
rodeo circuit to properly raise his toddler daughter. Problem
is, Pepper Bourne thinks his ranch belongs to her!

HWESTCNM0716

~Western ~Romance

Brady Sawyer almost died the last time he rode a bull, and now he's determined to compete again. Can surgeon Sheila Lindstrom risk her heart on a man who cares so little for the life she saved?

Read on for a sneak preview of
A BULL RIDER'S PRIDE,
the latest book in Amanda Renee's popular
WELCOME TO RAMBLEWOOD *series.*

"This can't happen again." Sheila squared her shoulders. "It happened, we got it out of our systems, we don't mention it to each other or anyone else. I could lose my job over that kiss."

"Then, you're fired."

"I'm what?" Sheila laughed. "You can't fire me as your physician, Brady."

"Actually, I can. You're telling me us being together is an issue because you're my doctor. I'm eliminating the problem."

"It's not that simple," Sheila said. "Grace General Hospital frowns on doctors dating former patients. I'd lose the respect of my colleagues. And if you run to my attending and have me removed as your doctor, it will raise a few red flags. I put my entire life on hold to become a doctor. I'm not throwing it away for a fling. Dedication and devotion from people like me are the reason you're alive today."

"Sheila, I respect your career. I admire your dedication and achievements." If she only understood that he'd devoted the same energy to his own career.

She scoffed. "You take everything for granted. I helped give you a second chance at life. A second chance to see your son grow up, and you want to throw it all away for pride."

"It's not pride. I have to earn a living to support my son." Brady sat down beside her. "Gunner is everything to me."

"Gunner doesn't care what you do for a living. He's four! He loves you no matter what." Sheila threw her hands in the air. "Okay, I'm done with this conversation. I don't care what you do." She stood and reached for the doorknob, then hesitated. She slammed her fist into her thigh. "So help me, I do care." She spun to face him. "That's the problem. I care what happens to you."

Brady hadn't expected Sheila to admit her feelings for him. He'd suspected and even hoped the attraction was mutual. But hearing the words, the connection between them took on a completely different meaning. How could he walk away from a woman who intrigued him like no other?

He reached for her hand. "This is all I know how to be—a bull rider. A rodeo cowboy."

"You're so much more than that," Sheila whispered.

Don't miss
A BULL RIDER'S PRIDE
by Amanda Renee, available August 2016 wherever
Harlequin® Western Romance
books and ebooks are sold.

www.Harlequin.com

*Wrangle Your Friends for the
Ultimate Ranch Girls' Getaway*

DISCARD

**Win an all-expenses-paid 3-night luxurious
stay for you and your 3 guests at
The Resort at Paws Up in Greenough, Montana.**

Retail Value $10,000

**A TOAST TO FRIENDSHIP,
AN ADVENTURE OF A LIFETIME!**

Learn more at
www.Harlequinranchgetaway.com

Sweepstakes ends August 31, 2016

WCHMR